Matt

Viṣṇu-rāta Vijaya

The Story of An Ex-Hunter

Stories of Devotion

Viṣṇu-rāta Vijaya

The Story of An Ex-Hunter

by

Satsvarūpa dāsa Goswami

(art by Yadupriyā-devī dāsī)

GN Press, Inc.

Persons interested in the subject matter of this book are invited to correspond with our secretary:

GN Press, Inc.
R.D. 1, Box 837-K
Port Royal, Pa 17082

Printed in the United States of America

ISBN: 0-911233-89-X

Author's Note

This story is inspired by a section in Lord Caitanya's teachings to Sanātana Gosvāmī, as found in *Caitanya-caritāmṛta*. In the *Madhya-līlā* chapter, "Explanation of the Ātmārāma Verse," Lord Caitanya tells the story of Nārada Muni's conversion of the hunter, Mṛgāri, into a first-class Vaiṣṇava.

Śrīla Prabhupāda compares Mṛgāri's breaking the animals' legs and leaving them half-dying, to the killing of millions of animals daily in modern slaughterhouses. As Nārada warned the hunter that he would have to suffer in retaliation for his cruelty, so Śrīla Prabhupāda warns the so-called civilized people who support the activities of the slaughterhouse. "They consider themselves very advanced in education, but they do not know about the very stringent laws of nature." Not only the killers in the slaughterhouse must suffer unlimited pains in the future, but also those who give permission to the slaughterers, those who transport the meat, those who cook it, who serve it, and who eat it.

Even people who are apparently not connected to these acts suffer when humankind faces reactions to animal killing. Reactions come in the form of war and natural disaster, and they are dictated by the laws of material nature. Śrīla Prabhupāda writes, "Who is safe? Who is happy? Who is without anxiety?"

Śrīla Prabhupāda's commentaries to the story of Nārada and the hunter also stress that Lord Kṛṣṇa maintains those who surrender to His devotional service under the direction of a pure devotee. Thus, the hunter, under the influence of Nārada Muni, abandoned his occupation, took fully to chanting Hare Kṛṣṇa, and became a non-violent, fully satisfied devotee of the Lord. Śrīla Prabhupāda has referred to Nārada and the hunter in his lectures. Devotees have also performed dramatic skits of the famous story, and Śrīla Prabhupāda witnessed one of them. I am therefore following the *paramparā* by elaborating on the original theme as a way to praise Lord Kṛṣṇa and the Vaiṣṇava *saṅga*.

When my readers turn to the "Translator-Editor's Preface," they may think that I am unnecessarily adding fictional devices. Instead of only Nārada and the hunter, we now have a friend of Mṛgāri's (who is only hinted at in the *Caitanya-caritāmṛta*—"All the villagers brought alms and presented them to the Vaiṣṇava who was formerly a hunter . . . ") and now there is an anonymous ancient biographer who has written the life story of Mṛgāri's friend. I have not made these additions in order to play inventor of reality. I am not the controller of this material, but only one of many authors or story-tellers who join together whenever the narration of Nārada and the hunter is told. And I am merely the latest and most insignificant to tell this eternal tale.

This is the nectar of Kṛṣṇa conscious writing: One joins the *paramparā,* humbly serves the previous *ācāryas* and repeats what they have said to new audiences. Śrīla Prabhupāda once advised the contributors of *Back to Godhead* magazine, "All students should be encouraged to write some article after reading *Śrīmad-Bhāgavatam, Bhagavad-gītā,* and the *Teachings of Lord Caitanya.* They should realize the information, and they must present their assimilation in their own words. Otherwise, how they can be preachers?" (letter, July 1, 1969).

Kṛṣṇa consciousness is overflowing; it wants to be told again and again, always faithful to the spirit of the original source. But it sometimes wants to be presented as "old wine in new bottles." Whenever a fallen soul comes into contact with the nectar of Vaiṣṇava activities and Vaiṣṇava story-telling, he too overflows with nectar and wants to express it in many ways, as freely as possible, "as if he possessed five mouths."

May the Supreme Lord have mercy on this story-teller and his audience, so that the narration will be protected both from deviations and from unnecessary criticism. May we enter the realm of literature in pursuance of the Vedic version and become free from birth and death.

—SDG, 1991

Translator-Editor's Preface

The ancient manuscript, *Viṣṇu-rāta Vijaya,* which is the life of Viṣṇu-rāta, was written in the now dead language of the aborigines of India. The anonymous author also uses frequent colloquial expressions difficult to understand now that we are so removed from that time. Therefore, I have taken the liberty of making a free rendering into modern English, instead of attempting an exact translation. The spirit of the original is intact.

The author appears to be a witness of many of the events in the life of Viṣṇu-rāta, and therefore, the work is concurrent with the appearance of the great Vaiṣṇava Mṛgāri, who was a direct disciple of the eternal Nārada Muni. Viṣṇu-rāta was a direct disciple of Mṛgāri; therefore, all the events described in *Viṣṇu-rāta Vijaya* occurred in what modern historians calculate to be the prehistoric epoch.

I have not translated this work merely out of intellectual curiosity; neither am I trying to serve the purposes of academic institutions. Viṣṇu-rāta* was a devotee of Lord Kṛṣṇa, as am I, and although his name is not recorded in any of the lists of disciplic succession as we have received them, he was consumed by the desire to carry out the instructions of his spiritual master during his lifetime. His opposition to the killing of animals is outstanding when

---

* Viṣṇu-rata was given the name "Fierce Killer" at birth, but the original biographer has preferred to call him Viṣṇu-rata throughout. (Vaiṣṇava-dāsānu dāsa)

we remember that he was born and trained to be an "enemy of the animals." The story is like a footnote to the śāstric narration of Nārada Muni and the hunter, Mṛgāri.

Although there is no evidence that Viṣṇu-rāta ever had the *darśana* of Nārada Muni, yet he is, to my mind, an inspiration for us commonfolk in Kali-yuga who are so prone to violence and degradation. The need to protect animals is much greater now than it was in former times, and nowadays, humanity (or should we say inhumanity) appears intent on devouring all life on the planet, either by consuming it, bombing it, or poisoning it. For this reason alone, a translation of *Viṣṇu-rāta Vijaya* is relevant in the 20th Century.

Mundane scholars will not only doubt the great antiquity of this work, but they will even doubt the historical existence of *Viṣṇu-rāta Vijaya*. In fact, the *paśandi* scholars do not accept even the reality of Nārada Muni and the Vedic civilization. But we are not concerned with mundane judgements here. I cannot definitely attest to the historical authenticity of this ex-hunter's story. What I am certain of is that an ancient manuscript was found in an equally ancient temple in North India. The manuscript deals accurately with the events described in the *śāstras* in relation to the story of Nārada and Mṛgāri. Whether we accept *Viṣṇu-rāta Vijaya* as history or as fiction, it is a work of devotion, seriously treating the themes of *ahīṁsa*, Vaiṣṇava *saṅga*, and *hari-nāma*. Therefore, it is worthy of our attention.

—Vaiṣṇava-dāsānu dāsa, New Delhi, 1991

Viṣṇu-rāta Vijaya

1

Viṣṇu-rāta's father, Paśu, gave his son the name "Fierce Killer" at birth (but as his disciple, I prefer to call him Viṣṇu-rāta throughout). As the son of a hunter, Viṣṇu-rāta was raised as a meat-eater and an animal-killer. His father practiced the half-killing of animals which Viṣṇu-rāta was to condemn later in his life. He said that those who practice the torture of animals are unaware of their own deaths and the subsequent punishment of being killed in a similar way.

In his old age, Viṣṇu-rāta sometimes recalled his childhood. His followers have written it down. "My father did not think half-killing was evil. He learned it from others and considered it a sport. It was also used to keep captured animals from escaping or from becoming carrion for crows and vultures before the hunter could return and claim his kill. He rarely spoke of God and knew nothing of karma."

As a boy, Viṣṇu-rāta was physically and mentally fit. He helped his father skin the day's catch, and upon reaching the age of five, he occasionally accompanied his father to the forest to witness the killing of small animals. His mother made him deerskin apparel, just like the dress all hunters wore. There is no use conjecturing about how one who later became pure-hearted and active in the cause of non-violence was so violent in his childhood. We are cautioned: *vaiṣṇavera kriye mudrā vijñe na bhujhaya,* one should not try to know the mind of a Vaiṣṇava or inquire into his previous life. I therefore do not wish to dwell on the details of his boyhood as a hunter. Neither did he tell us much about it. One can surmise, if one likes, the nature of Viṣṇu-rāta's childhood by seeing the lives of other aboriginal hunters. They are convinced that they *must* kill animals in order to sustain themselves. This was one of the important points addressed by Nārada in his conversion of Mṛgāri: One certainly can live without meat; Bhagavān Śrī Kṛṣṇa maintains all human beings without their having to devour innocent creatures who are also His children.

One cannot write about the life of Viṣṇu-rāta without feeling the sadness and wrongness of the hunters' lives—and the misery they cause themselves and others.

His father was pleased with Viṣṇu-rāta's early development. The boy took naturally to life in the woods. He learned to track animals and to be quiet and patient. He liked handling the bow and arrow and practiced it, easily grasping the rudiments of archery. As with any very young boy, he wanted to please his father and to learn what he was taught. But there were some early signs of what was to come later. He sometimes befriended animals. One time, a sparrow flew into the hunter's cottage and was fluttering through the three rooms, trying to get out. The hunter's wife tried to kill it with a broom but was unable. Suddenly, Viṣṇu-rāta said, "Don't bother, Mother." He then went up to the bird, spoke to it in a kind of baby talk, and extended his finger for the bird to perch on. The bird responded and jumped onto the boy's finger. He then walked to the open window, and allowed the bird to fly away. This incident pleased his father because he took it that the boy had a way with animals. This would be useful in the forest in his stalking practice.

Yes, he did kill animals under his father's order. What can be said, except as the *śāstras* tell us, no one should become a father or mother unless they can free their dependents from death? It is another burden to the already staggering karmic load of a hunter's life, that he trains his subordinates to be killers also. He sits them down to dinner and serves them the flesh of the rabbit and deer that he slew. On his order, his wife cooks it, and his little children dine on it in trust. He assures them that this is perfectly normal and that man was meant to live this way.

Viṣṇu-rāta later recalled that he once asked his father why killing animals was necessary. His father replied that if man did not kill them, then the animals would overpopulate the earth. Then he concluded, "Don't ask why, just do your duty."

Paśu also taught Viṣṇu-rāta to disregard hermits, *yogīs,* and devotees whom the hunters often found in the forest. He described them as crazy men who did not work to earn their living. (One had to be careful though, not to mistake a hermit for an animal and shoot him with an arrow, because the king would avenge the hermit.) But if such false sages ever encumbered a hunting expedition by their presence or habits—such as singing and frightening the animals away—they should be admonished and chased away. One just had to be careful in dealing with the hermits because some of them were known to possess "magic powers." They could curse an offender. This was the ignorant vision of *sādhu-saṅga* that the father imparted to his son.

Viṣṇu-rāta related much later in his life that he sometimes had friendly exchanges with forest *sādhus* when his father wasn't around. He was attracted to their clean, simple hermitages, and their singing and chanting, although he did not know what it was.

Viṣṇu-rāta once recalled that when he was a young boy, his father had a confrontation with a forest *sādhu.* The man came to the hunter's cottage asking alms, and the hunter cursed and drove him away. He told his family that these holy men were all useless parasites. The *sādhu* was tall and thin with a grey beard and an old white *dhotī* on his spare limbs. He had a merry look in his eyes

and merely smiled when he was driven away. It was embarrassing to little Viṣṇu-rāta to see his father behave like this, but he had to accept it as his father's way. Paśu said that the sages actually did not need food—they preferred to eat in the woods—

but they came begging as an excuse to preach their religion. It was right to drive away such meddlers.

Later, they encountered that same sage in the forest. Viṣṇu-rāta found him while scouting for wild boar on behalf of his father. The sage was sitting in meditation under a small lean-to of dead logs and branches. Viṣṇu-rāta was in his own mood of concentration, following the boar's spoor, and he came to observe the sage before he himself was seen. The sage was performing some prayer ritual before a stone, offering it flower petals, bowing down, and singing softly. The sunshine filtered onto the scene, and Viṣṇu-rāta observed that small birds and squirrels were playing fearlessly just a few feet away from the hermit. He appreciated that the hermit had such a friendly intimacy with the forest, whereas Viṣṇu-rāta was out to kill. How strange it seemed to the boy that the hermit could sit so peacefully, doing "nothing," looking so satisfied, and attracting the other creatures. Viṣṇu-rāta wondered for the first time in his life what the sages were actually doing. It didn't really appear to be "nothing" or nonsense as his father had told him. It seemed to be something interesting and mysterious and it caused no harm. Finally, the ritual complete, the sage looked up and silently motioned to Viṣṇu-rāta to come forward. He picked up some sweets he had placed on a leaf and offered one to Viṣṇu-rāta, who gladly took it and ate it. Suddenly, there was a crackling of twigs and Paśu stepped heavily into the clearing, glowering.

"Don't mess with my boy!" the hunter said, looking mean, but a bit wary, fearful of the sage's power.

"He came to me," said the hermit. "Hare Kṛṣṇa."

"Hare Kṛṣṇa yerself," said the hunter. "Whaddya give him? Give it to me."

"Nothing," said the sage. And when the father turned to his boy, Viṣṇu-rāta confirmed, "Nothing, Father." Thus Viṣṇu-rāta and the sage sealed a kind of secret trust, an exchange the boy never forgot. Suspecting he was being made a fool of, Paśu angrily kicked over the sage's small altar. The holy man cried out and began to recite fervent prayers. Paśu quickly led his son away, afraid he had gone too far, but telling Viṣṇu-rāta, "See how foolish they are!"

There have always been many Viṣṇu temples in Bharata-varśa. When Viṣṇu-rāta was growing up, he sometimes saw some of these temples, although he was not allowed to enter them.

It is not easy to become a devotee of Rādhā-Kṛṣṇa. It is likely to take hundreds of births. Kṛṣṇa says in the *Bhagavad-gītā* that only after many lifetimes as a philosopher can one reach the conclusion, "*vāsudevaḥ sarvam iti:* Lord Vāsudeva is everything." Worship of Lord Viṣṇu or Lakṣmī-Nārāyaṇa is not as complete as the worship of Rādhā-Kṛṣṇa; even "official" or nominal worship of Rādhā-Kṛṣṇa is not the same as real devotion in *kṛṣṇa-prema*. Real love is very rare. It comes only when one can meet and receive the mercy of a devotee who is deeply immersed in *kṛṣṇa-prema*. If one renders service to such a pure devotee, one can attain a connection with pure Kṛṣṇa consciousness. Viṣṇu-rāta was to meet a Vaiṣṇava when he was seventeen years old. There were some signs that Viṣṇu-rāta was ready to meet Kṛṣṇa, and that he had rendered service, although unintentionally, at the feet of the Vaiṣṇavas. For example, in the incident we just narrated, it appears that he took *mahā-prasādam* from a worshiper of a Kṛṣṇa-*śila* and had also been prepared to protect him by lying when confronted by his father.

In later reminiscences, Viṣṇu-rāta said that he saw the form of Kṛṣṇa in his childhood, Kṛṣṇa with His flute and Rādhārāṇī by His side, holding a flower. One small roadside temple had its door almost always open, and you could see Rādhā-Kṛṣṇa from the street as you walked by. He and his father often trudged past that place, sometimes carrying carcasses. When the boy was still known as "Fierce Killer," he saw pious people lie down in the road and call out, "Rādhā-Govinda *kī jaya!*" He remembered his father sarcastically mimicking them, "Rādhā-Govinda *kī jaya,*" and he liked to say it too, as play.

There were other temples in the neighborhood—Hanumān, Ganeśa, Sarasvatī, Mahādeva Śiva. Paśu once went to have a goat killed at a Kālī temple at the insistence of his wife, but he complained that it was too much bother and refused to do it again. He preferred to kill his domestic animals himself, without the trouble of paying a priest or being lectured about karma.

When he was seven years old, there was some controversy surrounding Viṣṇu-rāta's schooling. Paśu was against it ("Whoever heard of a hunter going to school? That's for *brāhmaṇas.* Let *me* teach him how to kill a tiger. Is some cowardly *sādhu* going to teach him that?"). But his mother was in favor: "He might learn something useful which will bring us some money. Mother Dūrga knows we need it. What if you have another bad winter like last year when all your skins were stolen?"

So they compromised, and Viṣṇu-rāta went twice a week to classes held in the village by a poor *brāhmaṇa.* When his father heard that the lessons included Sanskrit, he stomped out of the room, grumbling that it was a complete waste of time.

School attendance was another hint indicating the fortune that was yet to come to Viṣṇu-rāta. No hunter boys ever studied Sanskrit. Few hunter boys went to school at all. We cannot help but think that this was an arrangement by Providence so that later Viṣṇu-rāta could relish the Sanskrit *Vedas* with his spiritual master.

Viṣṇu-rāta later recalled only a few fragments from his school experience. In Sanskrit class, they heard a story about Vālmikī, the author of *Rāmāyāna,* which had a lasting effect on "Fierce Killer." Vālmikī had been a thief and killer, but one day, Nārada Muni told him about the law of karma. Nārada said that the killer would have to suffer punishment in a future life. This killer then asked his wife and children if they would share his karma, since he was stealing and killing in order to buy them food. But his family members said no, they would not accept his karma. The thief then surrendered to Nārada, who instructed him to chant the names of God. The thief regretted that he was too sinful. Nārada, in his wisdom, told him to meditate on all the death he had caused by chanting *marā, marā, marā.* As the thief and murderer began to chant, he realized he was actually chanting the holy name of Rāma. When Viṣṇu-rāta heard this, he wondered—for the first time in his life—if killing *animals* was something bad. Would he, his father, and the other hunters be punished? Yet they were only performing their occupational duty. But that thief who became Vālmikī was also doing his duty. Still, there *was* a difference because Vālmikī killed people whereas Viṣṇu-rāta killed animals.

That night, when his mother asked Viṣṇu-rāta what he had learned at school, he did not tell her the Vālmikī story. It was the first time he had ever kept something like that to himself. But he sensed that his parents would not be able to give him a fair hearing, and that his father might get angry if he heard the boy's doubts about hunting.

I cannot claim that Viṣṇu-rāta's childhood was all *līlā* or divine activity. He said that he was in illusion until he met his spiritual master. As the Vaiṣṇavas pray, "I was standing in the darkness of ignorance with my eyes shut, and my spiritual master forced open my eyes with the torchlight of knowledge." We offer obeisances to the guru because he has saved us from *māyā*. There is nothing shameful in being saved—actually, it is glorious.

Yet why tell of the māyic childhood, the animals he killed with bow and arrow, his inability to enter Vaiṣṇava temples, the long years of his childhood wasted with no utterance of the holy names? I tell of Viṣṇu-rāta, even in his childhood, because he is a genuine person. He was, in one sense, the same as all of us—engrossed in sinful life, ignorant of his sinfulness, and the recipient of a Vaiṣṇava's mercy. Hearing of his past can give us all the hope we require to continue in our own attempts to associate with the Vaiṣṇavas.

And I tell of these past events because he is my spiritual master. His childhood is endearing to me, even if he appears to be under the cloud of *tamo-guṇa*. Viṣṇu-rāta was not in ignorance; he was a pure soul (as we all are). Like all of us, he has been under the illusory cloud. To see his cloud-covered state brings us to a fuller appreciation of the full sunshine of guru's grace.

His mother was kind to him in her own way. She wanted him to be a good hunter. But is it possible to be a "good hunter"? You may be an expert killer of animals, or a prosperous trader in animal skins, or even an animal killer who can refrain from debauchery, but a *good* hunter is a contradiction in terms. When one becomes good, clean *(śucī)*, and fixed in transcendental knowledge, kind and equal to all living beings, then one ceases to be a hunter.

One day, in a moment of intimacy, he told his mother about the Vālmikī story. She immediately admonished him not to tell his father. She half-stated that perhaps it was possible he could grow up to be something other than a hunter, but she also asserted that there was really no fault in hunters killing animals if the proper sacrifices were performed for purification. Since Paśu did not perform the appropriate rituals to Goddess Dūrga, she was praying on his behalf to the goddess. By her rituals, she was protecting the family from any sinful reactions.

When he was very small and his parents served him meat at mealtimes, Viṣṇu-rāta did not at first realize the connection between the sliced food on his plate and the living creatures from whom the meat came. It was "veal cutlet" or "tongue" or "liver," and on holidays, his mother would prepare special dishes of curried "chicken." His mother would hold a big platter in her arms and serve him, smiling down at him as he ate with relish. Sometimes "gravy" was served, and even "blood." Drumsticks, fish soup, bacon, sausages, stew, ham, wishbones, frogs' legs, crabs—none of it evoked a sense of living creatures in the mind of Viṣṇu-rāta, and neither did his parents present it in that way. They did not try to hide it, but their concern was how it tasted, how it had been cooked and seasoned.

"Mmm, this is good steak," said his father. "These are tender, thick pieces. Give me some more blood on it. Eat up, Fiercy. Do you have enough?"

The boy would nod and exercise his young molars, munching and salivating on the juicy steak.

Sometimes, as dinner conversation, Paśu might mention what parts of the animal the meat had come from, yet when he said breast or thigh or wing, it was somehow remote from the living creature that walked or ran or flew. Even words like brain or eye or ear or foot never conjured up images of pain given to others, and certainly nothing about "bad karma" for those who ate meat. Meat came from animals—his father was a hunter—but he had never made the connection in an emotional way. It never disturbed him. Rather, dinnertime was an occasion when Viṣṇu-rāta's father was more congenial, and the whole family drawn together in loving union. "Eat up, Fiercy, did you get a good piece?"

"Give your mother some tender meat. She worked hard to cook this for all of us."

And Fiercy joined in the fun. At big holiday times like Dūrga-*pūjā,* when relatives would join them, he would ask his mother, "How much did the chicken weigh? What about the lamb?" He had heard other boys say that their families served six-pound or eight-pound chickens, and he liked it when his own family feasted on an eight-pounder. Some meat he didn't like, such as liver, but only because it seemed to have an obnoxious taste. They didn't have to force him to eat his ham on the thick slices of bread.

He lost his innocence one day while playing in a neighbor's yard. His friend's father came out, grabbed a live chicken, and chopped off its head with an ax. The action was so sudden and horrible—the bird's blood gushed out and the headless chicken ran in circles—that the little friend of Viṣṇu-rāta began to scream. The boy's father laughed. "What's the matter?" he chided his son. "Why you crying? Look!" And just to harden his son's sensibilities, the father grabbed another clucking chicken, wrenched its neck, and severed its head with his hatchet. Viṣṇu-rāta was about five years old at the time, and when his friend screamed even louder in horror, he cried and ran home to hide.

After that incident, Fiercy tried to avoid meat. "No thank you, I don't feel well," he said, when his mother offered him slices of meat. He thought of the cows and calves eating grass in the sunshine. He thought of the ghastly scene he had witnessed and wondered, *how do they kill a cow, with a big axe?*

Of course, this refusal was not allowed. Gradually, his mother and father got him to confess what troubled him. His father was disgusted and short-tempered to hear it. He told Viṣṇu-rāta's mother, "Beat some sense into him or I will. I don't want to hear this again." And so his mother took him aside after mealtime.

"Why don't you want to eat your supper?"

"Because I saw the chicken getting killed. Bala's father cut its head off and it was running around and around. It was really scary."

"There is nothing to be afraid of. The animals are already dead when we eat them. This is just good food. It is provided by the gods."

"But that chicken didn't want to die," said Fiercy.

"Well, everyone has to die. One living creature is food for another. These are the laws of nature, my son. Some things may not be so pleasant, but life is like that. You have to grow up and face it."

"But why did he have to laugh when he killed the chicken? It was horrible! Do the forest *sādhus* eat meat?"

His mother smiled. Such a precocious, inquiring child. "The hunters are like that," she said. "They have to be fierce because sometimes they have to kill ferocious animals. The *sādhus* may not eat meat, but you are not a *sādhu.* You are a hunter's son. Don't let your father hear you asking such questions again. And don't cry about the chickens."

Gradually they forced him to overcome his scruples about meat. His mother said it was absolutely necessary for his health. There was no question of his refusing. So he chewed and swallowed and didn't ask questions, but now he didn't do it without thinking. He couldn't forget that beef meant a cow had been killed, and bacon came from a slaughtered pig. The chickens running in the road would each be killed and eaten. After the incident, he no longer liked it when they served venison. Venison meant a pretty deer had been killed and sliced and cooked. He tried to put vivid thoughts out of his mind at mealtime.

But gradually he hardened his heart. He was a hunter's son and scruples about meat-eating were not allowed. The questions had all been answered by his mother: "The animals must be killed; everyone eats some living creatures. We are not *sādhus.* If you don't eat you will die. Don't speak like that again, you hear me?"

Viṣṇu-rāta began to see that meat-eating was something necessary. One ate meat and lived in the world where people kept chickens and cows, deciding at their births their purposes in the scheme of things. Animals were fattened and killed by butchers or by their own keepers. The animals may not like it, but it was necessary for the survival of the human race.

Viṣṇu-rāta lived with his new "knowledge of life," but he had yet to realize that he too was expected to kill the animals. It was his occupation, his *varṇa*, his *dharma*. He had seen his father bringing home dead animals even before the scene with the chicken getting its head cut off. He had assisted his father with tanning, but as he grew older, he was expected to do more, and gradually the implications dawned on him. He was learning to track animals and to use the bow and arrow, spear and knife, because he too would be a hunter.

Viṣṇu-rāta probably killed some small animals as a very young boy, but the outstanding incident that survived in his memory was the killing of his first ferocious animal.

It was a wild boar. These animals are distinct from village hogs—they are larger and tusked, and they will charge anything that crosses their path if they are in the mood.

When Viṣṇu-rāta was about eleven years old, a particularly large boar was terrorizing the goat herds in his village. This was unusual behavior for a boar, and the village people were convinced that the boar was either mad or possessed by some evil demon trying to wreak vengeance on them for some unknown sin. Although many hunters had suddened upon this boar in the forest, no one had been able to kill it. This only added to the fear that this boar was a demon incarnate, and when the boar killed a *sādhu* who was sitting in meditation just inside the forest, the villagers were convinced.

The villagers called a meeting to decide what to do about the boar. There were vivid descriptions of the boar's long tusks and razor-sharp hackles. Some of the hunters had been close enough to see the yellow coat of hair underneath the boar's stiff bristles, but none had been able to pierce it with an arrow. Some of the villagers suggested special *pūjās* to Goddess Kālī. She was the goddess who had been offended, they thought, and it was she who had to be propitiated in order to free themselves from this demon. Paśu scoffed. He stood up and addressed the crowd of villagers, "Let's form a party of hunters. This boar's just crazy. Maybe no other hunter has been able to kill it, but *I* have not tried. We don't need *pūjā*, we need courage."

So the next day, the hunters formed three parties under the direction of Paśu. Although most of the hunters were usually brave men, men who could face ferocious tigers, most of them were afraid of the boar. They insisted on performing a *pūjā* before the hunt to protect them from the boar's demonism. They called in a village tantric, who performed some magical rituals using the parts from a freshly slaughtered pig under a tree at the edge of the forest. Then he sprinkled them all with the blood from the sacrifice and danced wildly around the tree.

The party entered the forest at three different places, with plans to meet in a particular clearing near dusk. Viṣṇu-rāta accompanied his father's party. He was proud of his father's brave words, but still frightened by the demoniac boar. He tried to take his mind off his fear by becoming intent on looking for boar tracks on the path.

By midday, Paśu's party had come across two different packs of boars, but had not found the giant, lone boar they sought. Although the party had seemed concentrated all morning, when they broke for their noon meal, the hunters began to speak of the strangeness of the boar. How is it that so many expert trackers could not find a single animal? How had this boar managed to elude all their arrows when they had met it individually in the forest on previous days? As they talked, Viṣṇu-rāta could feel the ghostly presence of the boar close in on his mind. He began to perspire and look nervously about. What if right at this moment, while they talked, the boar was watching them from the bushes and preparing to charge? Is it over there? Viṣṇu-rāta could see the boar in his mind's eye—the small myopic reddish eyes, the raised hackles, the soft pink snout, the look of madness that possessed the boar—and he became infected with fear. Finally Paśu silenced the hunters, but he himself was looking nervously over his shoulder.

The party continued, but by dusk, when the three parties met in the jungle, no one had even sighted their quarry. They decided to go home. The forest was inhabited by many ghosts at night and no one, including Paśu, was willing to remain in the darkening trees.

As they set out for home, the boys were at a little distance from the men. Viṣṇu-rāta saw a turtle and began to follow it, watching the cumbersome way it moved. He was within earshot of the party, but now a line of trees separated him from them. Suddenly he saw the giant boar, half-hidden in the bush, looking at him. Viṣṇu-rāta was close enough to see its yellowish tusks, and for a moment, all the hunters' talks crowded into his mind. He could not move. He could still hear the tramping of the hunters as they made their way through the woods, silent now in fear of the night, but he could not find his voice to call out to them. The boar snorted and Viṣṇu-rāta shook himself. He grabbed his bow and two arrows from his back, and prepared for the boar's charge. The boar stepped out of the bush threateningly, and Viṣṇu-rāta released his arrow. It stuck in the boar's neck. The boar screamed. The boys heard it and came running with the men to the spot. They arrived just as the boar charged Viṣṇu-rāta, quickly covering the fifty feet between them. Viṣṇu-rāta discharged another arrow, which stuck in the beast's soft snout and frenzied it. The boar was running in circles, shaking its head violently, trying to dislodge the arrow. Blood was splashing everywhere. By now, Viṣṇu-rāta had run

Yadupriya dd.

behind a tree and was hastily climbing it. The boar charged again, urged on by its own pain, and Viṣṇu-rāta, unsheathing his knife, leapt upon the back of the boar and cut its throat. They were both covered

in blood as the boar, with Viṣṇu-rāta still on its back, rolled on its side in its death throes. As it died, a cheer went up among the hunters, and Viṣṇu-rāta felt himself being pulled away from the dead animal and embraced by his father.

"Damn, that's the best kill I ever seen!"

The whole party marched triumphantly back to the village, with Viṣṇu-rāta in the front. Although

it was dark when they reached the village, many torches were lit to see the big animal, and most of the people stayed up late talking about the day and its wonderful climax. Viṣṇu-rāta stayed up all night, refusing to wash the blood from his face, even though his mother had asked him to several times. He noticed for the first time the look of awe in the eyes of some of the young girls, and a few of them even came and spoke to him.

"Weren't you afraid?"

"Naw. I hardly had time to think. Anyway, no demon is a match for me!"

The killing of the wild boar was the end of Viṣṇu-rāta's innocence. After that, he regularly killed animals. These years were a high point in his relationship with his parents. He became more of a reliable assistant in the family affairs, and his parents several times mentioned to him that soon they would be making arrangements for his marriage.

I do not have any more data from this period of his life, from the years eleven to sixteen, so let us leave it. I am eager to tell of what comes next.

Just in case anyone is interested, I may submit here my own background in time and place. I was born ten years after Viṣṇu-rāta, in the same province of Bharata-varśa, but many miles distant from his village. I, of course, did not know him at this time, although as I grew up, I did hear a story of a boy who courageously killed ferocious animals, and perhaps that story came from Viṣṇu-rāta's village. I was not a hunter, but born into the family of a petty clerk. Although I was trained in languages and writing, I did not know anything of devotion to Lord Viṣṇu.

My heart was always empty. I knew only some priestly rites, business, and family affairs. I was being trained to be a scribe for writing out legal documents and religious books, but I never entered the spirit of life or love of God. I had only the official family guru that all children have, but no one to guide me on the path of *bhakti.* My parents were kind to me and cared for me materially, but they taught me that this lifetime was the all-in-all. God (if He existed), was there to fulfill our desires for this life or to supply us our necessities on the heavenly planets in the next.

I should not even write of my own life in this biography, but I am doing it to record the true glories of my Guru Mahārāja, Viṣṇu-rāta Gosvāmī. Since I later came to surrender to him as his disciple, I want to introduce myself as a player in the drama of his life. Many other persons awakened in Kṛṣṇa consciousness because of the activities and preaching of Viṣṇu-rāta Gosvāmī. He was a *sparśa-*

maṇi, a touchstone of devotional service. Viṣṇu-rāta himself became transformed by coming in contact with another amazing touchstone, the Vaiṣṇava formerly known as Mṛgāri—who directly received the strong embrace and liberating instructions from the greatest of all touchstones, His Divine Grace Śrīla Nārada Muni. That we will narrate in the next chapter.

2

I will now tell how a hunter named Mṛgāri became a great devotee, by the association of Nārada Muni. If this meeting did not take place, then there would be no Kṛṣṇa conscious life story of Viṣṇu-rāta. It was Mṛgāri, after he became a Vaiṣṇava, who became the spiritual master of Viṣṇu-rāta.

The story of Nārada and Mṛgāri is told in the oral histories.[*] I cannot improve on that narration, and I assume that my readers have already heard it. But I will retell it here briefly.

One time, the great sage Nārada Muni, after visiting Lord Viṣṇu in Vaikuṇṭha, was going to bathe at Prayāga, in the land of Bharata-varśa. While walk-

[*] This story has since been recorded in *Caitanya-caritāmṛta, Madhya-līlā,* Chapter 24, verses 229 through 282. (Vaiṣṇava-dāsānu dāsa)

ing on the forest path, he saw a sight that gave him great pain. A deer with its legs broken was flapping in pain. It had been shot by a hunter, but left half-killed. A little later on the path, Nārada saw other animals in this condition. Finally, he saw the culprit, a hunter, hiding behind a tree with a drawn bow.

Nārada went up to the hunter, and in so doing, he frightened the animal the hunter was about to kill. The hunter wanted to curse Nārada, but by the influence of the saint, he was unable to do so. He asked Nārada, "Why have you come off the path and scared my animals away like this?"

Nārada asked his own question: "Are you the one who leaves these animals half-killed, flapping in pain?"

The hunter replied, "Yes, I do. What's wrong with it?"

Nārada said, "It is bad enough when you kill animals, but it is much worse when you leave them half-dead, because you inflict greater pain on them. Listen, and please do me a favor."

The hunter felt charitable in the presence of Nārada and wanted to serve him. He said, "Yes, I will do you a favor, whatever you like. Let me give you some skins. I can even give you a deer or tiger skin."

Nārada said, "I am not interested in the skins. But I just want you to promise me that in the future, you will kill the animals. Don't half-kill them."

The hunter was astonished, "I don't understand. My father taught me to do this. When I leave an animal half-flapping in pain it gives me great pleasure, just as it was pleasurable to my father."

Nārada then told him that one who inflicted such pain on animals would have to suffer unlimitedly himself. Nārada briefly described the laws of karma: that the very animals the hunter tortured would, in the next life, come back and torture the hunter.

Hearing Nārada's strong presentation, and visualizing how it would happen in the future that the deer would come after him with its antlers, and that the other animals would come after him with various natural weapons to torture him, the hunter became somewhat convinced and fearful of what he was doing. He had never before spoken to a *sādhu* and become softened toward animals or moral teaching. This was an extraordinary circumstance because Nārada is so fully empowered by Lord Nārāyaṇa. Thus, the hunter, whose name was Mṛgāri ("the enemy of the beasts"), asked Nārada, "How can I be saved from these sinful acts?"

The hunter bowed down before Nārada and asked him to please become his guru. Nārada's first instruction was, "Break your bow and then I will tell you what to do." The hunter hesitated and said frankly that he did not know how he could live unless he used his bow as a livelihood. But Nārada said, "Don't worry, Kṛṣṇa will take care of you if you fully engage in devotional service." So with trust, the hunter followed Nārada's instructions.

Nārada then told him to build a very simple cottage and to spend all his time chanting Hare Kṛṣṇa and worshiping the *tulasī* plant. Mṛgāri was a married man, and Nārada encouraged him that both he and his wife could follow this simple plan of austere but blissful *sādhana.*

The hunter did as he was told by Nārada, and a wonderful transformation took place very quickly. The people of the nearby village came and were amazed to see how the once crude and horrible Mṛgāri was now so saintly. They started bringing food for him, and therefore, he had more than he needed.

After a considerable period of time, Nārada Muni happened to be traveling in the same area, this time with his friend, Parvata Muni. Nārada said, "I have a disciple near here. Let us stop and see him."

When Mṛgāri saw his spiritual master coming from a distance, he jumped up and happily ran toward his *guru mahārāja.* But then Nārada saw that Mṛgāri was making strange movements in his progress forward. Mṛgāri saw ants on the path and rather than crush them, he stopped to gently brush them out of the way. He finally reached Nārada and made his full *daṇḍavats.* Parvata Muni had observed the extreme care Mṛgāri took in not causing harm even to an ant, so he praised Nārada, "You are a touchstone because by your association, this once violent hunter has now become so saintly that he won't even harm an ant." Mṛgāri then invited the party of two sages to his humble home, and there, the ex-hunter and his wife served the pure Vaiṣṇavas *prasādam,* and danced and sang Hare Kṛṣṇa mantra just to please them.

Now I will tell of the first time Viṣṇu-rāta met Nārada-kṛpa Prabhu. I have read some accounts in the histories of Mṛgāri's conversion. He is not given any new spiritual name, but only referred to as "Mṛgāri" or "the hunter." But please don't blame me for giving him a name here. Since I have to describe him at length, I cannot keep calling him "the hunter." The essence of his spirituality is that he is a product of Nāradadeva's mercy; therefore, it is not so much that *I* have named him, but that he *is* Nārada-kṛpa.*

Let us begin our story.

Viṣṇu-rāta sometimes traveled on business for his family. There was a maker of bows in Prayāga, for example, who far excelled all others, and Paśu sent his son there occasionally to purchase bows

---

* As previously mentioned, there are many explanatory notes, digressions and intrusions into the story by our anonymous biographer. I am only occasionally sharing these with the reader, just to show you what I am up against in attempting to translate the work of such an effusive biographer. This explanation of the name "Nārada-kṛpa" also indicates that when the biographer does deliberately add something of his own to the life story, he lets us know it. And thus I have developed a trust in his narration—and an eye to see when he departs from history and gives us his whimsical self. (Vaiṣṇava-dāsānu dāsa)

and arrows. As a youngster, Viṣṇu-rāta traveled with his father to trade in skins for grains and cloth. But by his sixteenth year, Paśu often let him go with another boy his age, as long as not too much money or risk was involved. It was on one of these excursions that he came to the place where Nārada had bathed at the *tri-veṇī,* and where he had met Mṛgāri in the jungle. By the time Viṣṇu-rāta was seventeen years old, Mṛgāri had become Nārada-kṛpa dāsa and was well-established in his cottage, worshiping *tulasī* and continuously chanting Hare Kṛṣṇa.

Viṣṇu-rāta had no interest in all this, but his village friend and fellow traveler, Ambulal, was curious to meet the famous ex-hunter-turned-*sādhu*. Everyone in the village knew the ex-hunter and thought that he was wonderfully transformed by Nārada's grace. Many people flocked to see Nārada-kṛpa and honored him by giving alms. Most people were inclined to his sincere practice of renunciation, and they were always forthcoming with their offerings of respect. They were convinced that the ex-hunter was a bona fide worshiper of the holy name, and they held him in high esteem. But few hunters thought about it much. After all, what difference did it make to them if a single hunter broke his bow to sit down all day and chant mantras?

Viṣṇu-rāta was not much moved by Nārada-kṛpa's story. In one sense, he was amused that a low-class hunter could become the object of so much adoration. Hunters were usually looked down upon and considered outcastes by the pious folk of any village. But a hunter who deeply considered the implications of his trade? This was something hunters just didn't do, and it was unsettling to Viṣṇu-rāta's mind. Because Mṛgāri had given up his bow, should all other hunters do the same? Of course not. As Paśu had told him, "If we don't hunt, the world will be overrun by animals," and Viṣṇu-rāta added to that, "Animals and *sādhus.*"

Viṣṇu-rāta had completed his business, traded in skins and picked up excellent new bows and arrows for his father and himself, and bought a new cooking pot for his mother. He was ready to start immediately on the return journey. But his village friend, who was the son of a utensil maker, said, "It's late and too dark to start. Let's go in the morning. Tonight, let's go see this *sādhu,* Mṛgāri. I really want to see what all the excitement is about."

"Who cares for a *sādhu?* Let's go find something interesting to do." But Viṣṇu-rāta was not entirely opposed to the idea, and his friend persuaded him.

They had to inquire where Mṛgāri's cottage was from the villagers. They were sent some distance away from the village, to the bank of the holy river. It was a much smaller cottage than Viṣṇu-rāta's family home, more like a lean-to constructed from four logs as pillars and a roof of thatch. In front of the cottage was a blooming *tulasī* plant in a large, clay pot and set on a raised platform. As they arrived, the young men saw Mṛgāri's wife tending to the *tulasī,* and they heard the sound of the ex-hunter within his cottage loudly chanting Hare

Kṛṣṇa, Hare Kṛṣṇa, Kṛṣṇa Kṛṣṇa, Hare Hare/Hare Rāma, Hare Rāma, Rāma Rāma, Hare Hare.

Viṣṇu-rāta's curiosity was aroused. Since his father wasn't present, he could allow himself to feel a natural attraction for the peaceful scene. Mṛgāri's wife greeted them courteously, and encouraged them to water the *tulasī* plant with a small *ācamana* spoon sitting in a small brass water cup. Viṣṇu-rāta accepted the invitation. He had often seen people water the "sacred plant," but he had never done it himself. As he stood awkwardly after watering the plant, Mṛgāri's wife indicated that he should now offer obeisances. Viṣṇu-rāta, feeling a little foolish, got down on his knees and touched his head to the ground.

"May we see your husband?" Ambulal asked.

She opened the thatch curtain that hung in the doorway and they entered the cottage. Viṣṇu-rāta liked what he saw. The *sādhu* was strongly built, as befits a hunter, but he was not fierce or dirty as they usually are. He had marked himself with Vaiṣṇava *tilaka* and wore a plain white *dhotī.*

Viṣṇu-rāta surprised himself. He began inquiring from the ex-hunter-*sādhu.*

"So you were a famous hunter," said Viṣṇu-rāta. "What happened that now you have given it up and you are chanting mantras to Kṛṣṇa?"

"I did nothing special," Nārada-kṛpa Prabhu said to them. "I just happened to be on the path when

Yadupriya d.d.

the great saint Nārada came through the forest on his way to the *tri-veṇī.*"

"I've heard of Nārada Muni," said Viṣṇu-rāta. "He is the same one who converted the killer Vālmikī, who then wrote the *Rāmāyaṇa.*"

The ex-hunter smiled. "Yes! Nārada appears as the guru of many great and fallen souls."

The ex-hunter's wife entered and placed clay water cups before the two guests. A few other villagers had arrived, and seeing that a discussion was underway, sat quietly, their eyes fixed on Nārada-kṛpa Prabhu.

"But I thought Nārada was just someone written about in books," said Ambulal. "I thought he was someone who lived in the past or was only a myth."

"He is certainly written of in the books," said Nārada-kṛpa, "but he is definitely not a myth. I have seen him myself, so I can attest to that. He prefers to visit very great devotees and demigods like Lord Śiva and the Kumāras, but no one can check Nārada. If he likes, he can give his mercy even to an animal or to an animal-killer."

Viṣṇu-rāta's alert eyes took in everything. He noticed how neatly the ex-hunter had decorated his body with Vaiṣṇava *tilaka.* He also noted the mark on his shoulder from carrying the bow. He glanced around the small cottage and saw the gaze of reverence the villagers fixed upon the ex-hunter. And he saw the bare simplicity, the utter cleanliness of the room in which they sat. Viṣṇu-rāta sensed what a great opportunity it was that his father wasn't with him. He could for once talk freely. Questions seemed to be bursting out of his chest.

"What's wrong with killing animals?" he asked.

"That is the same question I asked Nārada when he stopped me," said Nārada-kṛpa. He answered every question while gazing steadily into Viṣṇu-rāta's eyes. He seemed confident, and yet not at all sarcastic or condescending.

"In fact, my question to Nārada was, 'What's wrong with *half-killing* the animals?' Nārada had seen me torturing animals. That was my habit. I used to break their legs and leave them flapping in pain. Then later I would come back and kill them. You are also a hunter?"

"My father is a hunter," said Viṣṇu-rāta, and he felt a twinge of pride. Thinking of his own exploits in the jungle he said, "I have also been hunting for over five years. It is a great adventure to match wits against all of nature, and it takes courage to hunt. It is my duty. The animals were placed here on earth for man to hunt for his food. We have to hunt to keep nature's balance, to prevent the animals from overpopulating the earth. What's your objection?"

"You are wrong if you think you must eat animal flesh in order to live," said Nārada-kṛpa. "This is a fallacy. I am much healthier now that I eat only vegetables, milk, fruits, and grains."

Viṣṇu-rāta had no response. It seemed obvious that what the ex-hunter said was true. He was the living proof. He had dismissed a huge argument in favor of killing animals in only a few words.

"The objection to killing is obvious but we cannot see it," said Nārada-kṛpa. "Human beings should not cruelly kill animals, or even worse, torture them and leave them writhing. What if you were to go through your village torturing children and women, breaking their legs and killing some. Do you think you could get away with that without being punished?"

"But that's a different case," interrupted Ambulal. "There is a difference between people and animals. There's no law against killing *animals*." Ambulal was near-sighted and he squinted as he spoke. He was not a hunter, and he was a little amused at Viṣṇu-rāta's growing intensity.

"In a God conscious state it is against the law," answered Nārada-kṛpa. "And even if this state does not enforce it, there are laws of God. Do you believe in the supreme law of God?"

"Well . . . " Viṣṇu-rāta stammered. He knew he was ignorant about the subject of God. "Which . . . which god do you mean?"

"I mean the God of gods, *deva deva jagat pate,*" Nārada-kṛpa said. "It is declared in *Bhagavad-gītā, Śrīmad-Bhāgavatam,* and in many other Vedic literatures that the Supreme Personality of Godhead is greater than all gods, who are actually His assistants. In His original form He is Kṛṣṇa, He expands as Viṣṇu, and He has demigods like Brahmā and Śiva. Have you read Kṛṣṇa's statements in *Bhagavad-gītā?"*

"No," Viṣṇu-rāta and his companion answered in unison.

"If you would like to hear what Kṛṣṇa says," said Nārada-kṛpa, "you can come here another time. My friends and I regularly read and discuss from the *Bhagavad-gītā*. Come when you can. Chant with us—and hear."

"We don't live nearby," said Viṣṇu-rāta. "We came to see the old man who makes bows in this village. Thank you anyway, but . . . " Viṣṇu-rāta was eager to get back to some of his main points. He still wasn't satisfied.

"So you say the objection to killing animals is that there's a law against it, a law of God? Is that the only objection?"

"That's a pretty big objection," said Nārada-kṛpa. "And it is not just an arbitrary law. God is just. He does not allow us to inflict cruelty on others. If we breach this trust He has given us, this higher intelligence, and use it to commit acts of violence even against animals, we will have to face terrible reactions of karma or punishment. Do not think in terms of a law that you are free to obey or disobey. As Nāradadeva showed me, a hunter is in real danger. At any minute, any one of us may die, and if you have on your head the karma of torturing many innocent creatures, then you will have to suffer in your next life. The same animals whom you tortured and killed will come back and torture you."

"I find that hard to believe." Viṣṇu-rāta's voice was filled with skepticism.

"You may believe or not believe," said Nārada-kṛpa. "Your belief is a different issue. But it is a fact."

Again Viṣṇu-rāta had nothing to say. He was not used to debates. Besides, he did not feel inclined to argue against this holy man, but instead to accept his words as true. Viṣṇu-rāta's mind stopped short of further argumentation. Maybe later he could consider the arguments more carefully and think over what the *sādhu* had said, but for now he was stumped. He *was* worried about the karma. Viṣṇu-rāta began to feel nervous. What would his parents say if they knew he had come here and heard these attacks on their life's work? There were many other questions he wanted to ask the ex-hunter-turned-Vaiṣṇava, especially about how he had managed to change his mentality and habits. Did he go against his parents when he became a Vaiṣṇava? How did Nārada actually convince him about the animals coming back in the next life to attack? What was Nārada like? Was the ex-hunter happy now? How could a person *dare* to change his occupation? What was the benefit of chanting Hare Kṛṣṇa all the time? How could you survive if you gave up your occupation, gave up your bow?

Although he very much wanted to ask these questions, Viṣṇu-rāta could go no further. He felt a return of his identity as a hunter, the return of power to his back and arms, the growing awareness of his senses being filled with the night sounds of the jungle. Nearby a hyena screamed, and it was answered by the loud roar of a lion. He suddenly felt embarrassed to be submissive before a *sādhu*. He was not foolish, and he was not a "holy man." He had had enough.

As Viṣṇu-rāta's questions abated, others in the room began to speak with Nārada-kṛpa.

"Your Grace, we have brought you some rice and *attar*," said a young husband, who was accompanied by his wife. "Please accept them in your devotional service."

Nārada-kṛpa nodded and said, "I think you have been sent by Nārada Muni. Years ago he said that he would personally arrange for people to bring me food. When I asked him how he managed to arrange this, he said it was actually Kṛṣṇa who promises that if you become His devotee, He will supply all your needs."

An older man in the room made an inquiry about how to improve in one's chanting of Hare Kṛṣṇa.

That discussion was over Viṣṇu-rāta's head and he could not concentrate on the reply. Distracted, he thought of his own situation. Nārada-kṛpa had emphatically stated that Viṣṇu-rāta was in great peril because of his hunting. How could he believe that? And what if he did accept it as at least possible? . . . He looked at the floor and then at the sage, and, furrowing his brow, he clenched and unclenched his fists. "There is nothing wrong with what I am doing," he told himself angrily. "If anything, this Mṛgāri has abandoned his own responsibility. He is wrong." He continued to replay his conversation with Nārada-kṛpa again and again until Ambulal nudged him and whispered, "Let's get out of here."

The two young men bowed and excused themselves from the company.

"Thank you very much for visiting me," said Nārada-kṛpa. "Please come again if you have time. You and I are already close because you are a young hunter and I was a hunter for many years. I think we have a lot in common." When he said that, Viṣṇu-rāta's anger dissipated. He thought, "Yes, we *do* have a lot in common," and he very much wanted to come again.

"We will try to come again," said Viṣṇu-rāta, and they went out into the night.

As they walked back to the town, Ambulal asked what he thought of the *sādhu*.

"He has a powerful presence," said Viṣṇu-rāta. "I would like to go back. What did you think?"

"I think your father would kill you if he knew you had visited this man."

Viṣṇu-rāta stopped walking and took the thin arm of his friend in his own muscular one.

"Then don't tell my father what happened tonight. He said some very heavy things and I need to think about them. Let's not tell anyone about it."

"I won't tell," said his friend. "I was also interested in the concepts, even though I am not a hunter. It's not just what he says, but his peacefulness and strength."

"Yes, yes, you saw it too. Of course."

Viṣṇu-rāta returned to his village and said nothing to anyone about his meeting with Nārada-kṛpa Prabhu. His father was pleased with the purchases from Prayāga. The next morning, Viṣṇu-rāta woke early as usual and headed alone into the forest for a dawn hunt. For a year now, he had been going hunting alone in the early morning, with his father's permission. And he had done well too. He had found that dawn and the hottest part of the afternoon were the best times to catch animals unaware and slowed down. He also seemed to possess special skill for stalking them when he himself was fresh.

But this morning was different. He was thinking about what Nārada-kṛpa had said about causing pain to animals and God's law. These things were so new to Viṣṇu-rāta that he didn't know exactly what to *do* with them. But he knew that he had gone out early, not only to hunt, but to be alone. He didn't want to talk further with his parents now. He was not in any condition to talk and act with them as if everything were the same.

Treading lightly so as not to crack even a twig under his feet, Viṣṇu-rāta entered the paths he knew so well. These paths were frequented by deer and other wildlife, and he quickly spotted deer droppings and fresh tracks. He saw a small clearing where the grass had been crushed, and he knew deer had spent the night there. He took his new bow off his shoulder and placed an arrow in it, then continued walking forward. A few birds had woken and were singing to usher in the morning. It was just after monsoon season and everything was very fresh. The *chameli* flowers were already closing and the fresh wave of fragrant *mogra* were blossoming in the sun. Grass was growing luxuriantly. Viṣṇu-rāta stopped for a moment; there was a crackling sound ahead. He had the ability to look in the exact direction from whence a sound came, and he could also approximate its distance. He heard it again and judged that it was not a very large animal. He crouched behind a tree and waited.

Out of the undergrowth came a tan-colored fawn. It looked like it was only a few days old and it walked forward on long, spindly legs. Viṣṇu-rāta immediately sized up the situation. Its mother must have left it in order to look for safe pasture ground, and then she would be back. His father would have instantly shot the fawn and broken its legs. The fawn would then sound out distress signals to its mother, and she would certainly rush back to defend her young. She would be easy prey for any hunter.

Normally, Viṣṇu-rāta carried out this procedure with measured calmness, and he would have prided himself on making such a kill. But this morning was different. Instead, he remained crouched behind a tree, as the fawn, whose senses were not well-developed, continued walking toward him. Viṣṇu-rāta wasn't thinking of anything in particular. He was mainly watching—observing the fawn, sensing the pulse of life in the forest, and seeing himself. Something had happened in his meeting with the *sādhu;* he felt different. Although his old self would have already leaped forward and done the job, he now felt compelled to simply observe the shaky efforts of the fawn to cross the small clearing and reach the jungle.

When the fawn came within thirty feet, Viṣṇu-rāta began to coo. No one had taught him how to do this, but he found himself doing it whenever he wanted to get close to animals. This fawn startled at the sound, stopped to sniff the air, but then continued walking toward him. Their eyes met and Viṣṇu-rāta coaxed the fawn forward with assuring nods and motions with his open hands. It was a pretty animal, with large eyes and a wet nose. It came right up to his hand and he touched its muzzle as if it were a calf in a barn. *It's just as easy as killing,* he thought.

The doe returned and noticed that her fawn was gone. She snorted with fear as she suddenly saw her offspring in the hands of the hunter. Viṣṇu-rāta had put down his bow and he now stood to face the big doe, who was about fifty feet away. She snorted several times loudly, threatening to attack. Viṣṇu-rāta decided to leave. He quickly picked up his bow and walked deeper into the forest.

Now he walked without his usual light-footed caution. On all sides, little animals fled from him in fear. They sensed that he was something especially to be feared. Squirrels ran up the trees and taunted him with chock-chock-chock sounds, warning the other animals. A bird that cried, *"few-few"* began screaming, and it was relayed to other *"few-few"* birds deeper in the forest. The alarm system went up—the hunter is coming! The hunter is coming! Viṣṇu-rāta saw all this in a way he had never experienced before. He saw that he did not really belong. Wherever he turned, every living creature was afraid of him. And he had always fancied himself to be "at one" with nature. Now he realized that he was not even at one with himself. *They are all afraid of you because you are a killer,* he said to himself. *You cause them great pain, leaving them flapping. You have caused them great pain. This is a sin. You are a sinner.* Viṣṇu-rāta felt like crying. He sat down on the forest floor, but he could not cry.

When he returned home late in the morning, Paśu was surprised that he had not killed anything. Viṣṇu-rāta only mumbled a reply that he had tried.

His father scoffed at him. "Hmph. Whadja do, just go out to smoke a *bidi* and fall asleep?"

Seeing her son looking dejected, Viṣṇu-rāta's mother intervened. "That happened to *you* also last week," she said to her husband. "I'm sure he'll catch something this afternoon, won't you, Fiercy?" Viṣṇu-rāta nodded a silent reply and walked into his room. But that afternoon, he did not go into the forest.

3

Viṣṇu-rāta wanted to return to Prayāga. He purposely broke one of his new bows and then insisted on going to the bow-maker to have the "faulty" bow replaced. Paśu was in agreement. This time, he traveled alone and went directly to the cottage of the ex-hunter. He bowed down before the *tulasī* and called out at the door of the cottage.

"I have to talk to you," said Viṣṇu-rāta impatiently. Nārada-kṛpa was glad to see him.

"How can a hunter maintain himself if he gives up the only occupation he knows?" Viṣṇu-rāta asked, almost belligerently.

"I can only tell you how Nārada Muni convinced me." Nārada-kṛpa Prabhu spoke quietly. "His first instruction to me was to break my bow. I asked him, 'Then how will I maintain myself?' He said, 'Don't worry, I will supply your food every day.' And it has happened. I thought that by killing and trading dead animals, *I* was earning my income, but now I realize that every living being—from the greatest to the smallest—is being maintained by the one Supreme Being, Kṛṣṇa, who maintains everyone. If you wish to be a hunter, it will *appear* that hunting is your source of income. If you become a poor *brāhmaṇa* and completely dependent on Kṛṣṇa, without conducting any business, *still* your maintenance will be supplied by Kṛṣṇa. It is not the bow that supports your life, it is Kṛṣṇa. Maybe you will get less to eat or more, or simpler food or better food, but you will live, maintained by Kṛṣṇa. In my case, everything has improved. My wife and I receive more food than we need, and we distribute some to others. Your occupation as a hunter is just a temporary designation. You do not know that you are spirit soul. When you die, will you still be a hunter? Your real occupation is to serve the Supreme Lord, and if you carry out *this* occupation, all your needs will be satisfied."

Viṣṇu-rāta reacted as if he had been slapped in the face. Not a hunter? Spirit soul? What is he talking about? If I won't be a hunter when I die, what will I be? His mind was racing, but he felt somehow assured by Nārada-kṛpa's quiet, patient voice.

"What is this chanting?" Viṣṇu-rāta asked. "Why do you chant?" He was moving quickly now, following the torrents of thoughts storming his mind.

"Because my spiritual master told me to," replied Nārada-kṛpa. "It's as simple as that. Chanting the names of the Supreme Lord is the best and only way for people to get a direct audience of Bhagavān

Śrī Kṛṣṇa, especially in this age of Kali. Kṛṣṇa appears in His name."

"You mean when you chant, Kṛṣṇa comes in a vision to your eyes?" Viṣṇu-rāta asked incredulously.

"Not a vision exactly," said Nārada-kṛpa, "although Kṛṣṇa can appear in any form He likes. But in chanting He appears in the sound. It is easy to make this sound, Hare Kṛṣṇa. You chant and Kṛṣṇa promises that He appears. If you will come and hear the scriptures with us, you will see that the glories of chanting Bhagavān's names, *hari-nāma,* are proclaimed without limit in all the *śāstras.* The holy name is a liberated sound vibration. It comes straight from Kṛṣṇaloka. When it touches your tongue, it transforms you from matter to spirit."

"All this happens right away?" Viṣṇu-rāta asked his questions without premeditation. He was not afraid that Nārada-kṛpa would judge him the way his own father did if he asked the "wrong" question.

"It begins to happen right away," said Nārada-kṛpa. "When you begin to chant, there are many imperfections. I have been chanting for a few years now, and I cannot yet control my mind. Sometimes thoughts from the past come and disturb me temporarily. But I go on chanting. Even the beginning stage, which is like the shadow of the holy name, brings you Kṛṣṇa's purifying presence—and the name relieves you of past sin. I am eager to go on chanting and experiencing the further stages. But basically, I am under the order of my *guru mahārāja,* Nāradadeva, and I am happy for the first time in my life. I feel great relief to have escaped from my former life as Mṛgāri, the enemy of the animals."

"Please tell me more about the chanting," said Viṣṇu-rāta. He felt himself on the verge of saying more, but if he had spoken his mind, it would have come out like an incoherent torrent. He was thinking, "I have lived in ignorance. I didn't even know I had a self other than this body, the son of a hunter. I don't know the scriptures and have practically never even heard of Bhagavān Śrī Kṛṣṇa. I have always harassed the devotees of the Lord. It never occurred to me that any of my behavior was wrong. Everything has been turned upside down. I am afraid of what is happening, but I am even more afraid to remain in ignorance. *I have never been happy. I have been very cruel to other living entities.* I think that you can understand my heart because you are a saintly person and also because you too were a hunter. You know what it's like to kill and to live in such ignorance."

Even without saying all this, Nārada-kṛpa could see it in the boy's eyes, and Viṣṇu-rāta sensed that Nārada-kṛpa was reading his thoughts. But it was necessary to select a question out of his incoherent sense of need. So Viṣṇu-rāta forced himself to ask one question at a time, and to hear the answers carefully.

"If you try the chanting yourself," said Nārada-kṛpa, "then Kṛṣṇa, who is in your heart, will teach you. My case was desperate, so Nārada recommended a complete change of life to create ideal conditions for chanting. But even if you add the chanting to what you are doing, it will work. I will be pleased to serve you in any way I can. I am here chanting all the time, and I will try to answer your questions according to my limited knowledge. But if you yourself chant, you will gain everything for yourself—peace, spiritual knowledge, courage, conviction. Kṛṣṇa is all these things and He is fully in His name—He can give all these things to you. I can see that you are sincere, so He will bless you with rapid advancement."

Viṣṇu-rāta was flattered that the sage thought him sincere. He would definitely try the chanting as the sage recommended. He anticipated that wonderful things would start to happen.

"What I fear most of all," said Viṣṇu-rāta, somewhat calmer, "is my father. If he knew that I had come here, he would be very angry and may even beat me. I have been afraid of him all my life." Viṣṇu-rāta suddenly broke down and began to cry. He began sobbing and big tears rolled down his cheeks. "Hunters don't cry," he told himself, but it overcame him anyway. Nārada-kṛpa and his wife sat with him silently, but their empathy was tangible. They had been through it and they were able to console him simply by their presence.

Finally he gained control of himself and wiped his eyes with his hands.

"Excuse me," he said. "It's all pent up." He touched his chest.

"I know," said Nārada-kṛpa.

"When I left here the other day," said Viṣṇu-rāta, "I went home and went out the next morning to hunt. But I couldn't kill the deer. I didn't tell my parents why. They would never understand. They want me to be brave, a hunter."

"And now you will have to be a brave devotee," said Nārada-kṛpa.

"Yes." Viṣṇu-rāta sat up straight just as the sage was sitting. He felt more relaxed now, as if Nārada-kṛpa had been his friend for a long time.

"You are right," said Viṣṇu-rāta, "I will have to be brave. This is harder than killing the tiger."

"*This* is your tiger," said Nārada-kṛpa.

Viṣṇu-rāta again wavered as he thought of his parents, "But how can I do it? How can I do something that is disobedient to my parents? I don't want to cause my mother pain. And my father will be so disappointed. He wants a son who will carry on his good name, a son he can be proud of. Should I really give up everything?"

"You don't have to do everything at once," said Nārada-kṛpa. "Start to chant. Chant with us today."

"And when I go home?" asked Viṣṇu-rāta. "It's hard for me to travel here very often. It's so far. And when I am away from you I might forget. Should I just leave my family home?"

"You are young," said Nārada-kṛpa. "Just start chanting. Kṛṣṇa will gradually reveal to you what you should do."

"But what about killing animals? Should I stop and never do it again? I mean, I have already stopped. How could I live with my father if I refused to hunt? What will I eat?"

Viṣṇu-rāta saw that his questions were difficult to answer, even for Nārada-kṛpa. He didn't want to demand that the sage solve everything for him. He knew that he had to work things out for himself. But how could he do it? Viṣṇu-rāta thought, "Maybe Nārada-kṛpa has already said what I need to know by telling me to brave. And he keeps saying that I should chant."

So Viṣṇu-rāta spent the day with Nārada-kṛpa. He began chanting Hare Kṛṣṇa for the first time in his life. They gave him *tulasī* beads and he sat near the *tulasī* plant on the bare earth, fingering the beads and chanting *japa*. His heart and mind were full of scenarios and plans—full of impatience too—but Viṣṇu-rāta persisted in the chanting and enjoyed it. He loved the grove they were in, with the palm trees and the black squirrels running about, and the colorful jungle birds. He loved the pious people who came to see Nārada-kṛpa, or to leave him something to eat, and he felt welcomed by them. He felt at home, and as he chanted, he tried to build up his will for the test ahead. He would have to start his journey home and confront his father. It wouldn't be easy, but Kṛṣṇa would be with him if he chanted His names.

"Where have you been?" his father asked. "Why haven't you killed anythin' in three days?"

Gradually Viṣṇu-rāta let it come out. He told his father that there was an ex-hunter in Prayāga who had become a Vaiṣṇava, and he had been talking to him.

His father had been eating, but he sat erect and glared. "What is he, a coward or somethin'? Why'd he give up huntin'?"

"He met the great sage, Nārada."

"There ain't no real person Nārada. That's just in books. I knew your head would get too full if we sent you to that damn school."

"No, Nārada's real, father. And this man met him. The villagers there saw it all. Nārada told him it's bad to kill, and it's worse to leave animals half-dead."

"That's garbage. You can do anything you want to an animal when you're huntin'. Nothin's bad. But I'll tell you what's bad—when your son runs off and doesn't do his duty. When he comes home with a cockeyed idea and thinks he's smarter than his old man, that's bad. When he becomes a coward and sissy and can't hunt, that's bad."

"Paśu, please don't be violent," said his mother.

"I'll say and do whatever I want in my house. If I want, I'll take my belt and beat this little wise-guy's ass."

"He's too old for that," said Viṣṇu-rāta's mother.

"I won't be insulted by no one." Paśu's voice was rising. "I don't care how old he is or if he is my

son." The father stood glaring at his son and said, "I say that you're a bum, that's what. And that bum in Prayāga is no better than the urine of a dog."

Viṣṇu-rāta flinched. "You're a dirty killer," he said to his father. "All you ever taught me was how to go to hell. And that's where you're going."

Paśu swung at him with his fist, and hit his son on the lip. Viṣṇu-rāta ran out into the backyard. He pulled out his knife and began slashing a week's collection of animal skins that were stretched out behind the house.

Paśu came out and howled when he saw what his son was doing. He ran back in the house and returned with his club.

Viṣṇu-rāta's mother was screaming.

Viṣṇu-rāta grabbed his own club and squared off with his father in the yard. The father struck but Viṣṇu-rāta parried the blow. Paśu was much stronger than Viṣṇu-rāta, but Viṣṇu-rāta was faster.

His mother had run to the neighbors for help, and now villagers were running in and grabbing both Paśu and his son.

"Get the hell outta my house!" Paśu screamed.

"Damn your house!" yelled Viṣṇu-rāta. "You are a torturer of animals and whoever lives with you is going to hell."

A policeman stepped forward. "Why did you hit him?" he asked Paśu over the din.

"All I did was visit the Vaiṣṇava, Nārada-kṛpa," Viṣṇu-rāta interrupted angrily. "What's so terrible about that?"

Some of the villagers knew of the ex-hunter and they agreed that he was a good person.

"And I'm a hunter," said Paśu, pushing himself against the restraining arms of his neighbors. "What's so terrible about that?"

"Nothing, nothing," said a townsman.

"Fiercy, you go over to my house" said the policeman, "and leave us with your parents. You are both acting like madmen."

Viṣṇu-rāta's heart was beating rapidly and his swollen lip was burning. His shirt was splashed with blood and he rubbed his chest again and again to calm himself down. After about an hour, the policeman returned home and sat with him. They were neighbors, and he had known Viṣṇu-rāta from his childhood. "A son should be tolerant of his father's anger," he advised. "It was wrong that you destroyed the skins. Everyone has their own occupation. You and your father are hunters. Even if an occupation has some fault, just as fire has smoke, that doesn't mean you should abandon it."

"But killing animals is sinful," said Viṣṇu-rāta.

"What do you mean by sinful?" the policeman asked. "If you want to grow up to be a *sādhu* and not kill animals, that's a different thing. I won't meddle in your life and in your relationship with your father—unless you start fighting again. But just because a *sādhu* doesn't kill animals doesn't mean no one else in the world can kill animals. Do you understand?"

Viṣṇu-rāta didn't want to pursue it with him. Neither had Nārada-kṛpa Prabhu ever hinted that he should curse his father or destroy his animal skins. "That was my own hate," thought Viṣṇu-rāta, and he felt that he had plenty more of it inside. He also felt a resentment that his father had raised him to kill and torture. With so many emotional thoughts, Viṣṇu-rāta was bewildered. He felt that the whole foundation of his life was cracking like an earthquake.

The policeman gave him hot *kichari* and told him to sleep overnight on the porch. He also instructed him to go home in the morning and, in a humble mood, make amends with his parents. Viṣṇu-rāta slept fitfully. He woke early and decided to go into the forest before sunrise. Walking quickly through the empty village streets, he went home and snuck into his room. His parents always slept late, so he knew he was safe from confrontation. Taking his spear, he headed for the forest.

He sighted a few deer, but he was not interested in them this morning. He was hunting boar. By reading the forest signs, he found a pack of male boars, supervised by a big male pig.

Viṣṇu-rāta picked off one of the smaller boars by poking it with his spear and driving it apart from the others. When the big boar saw this, it charged Viṣṇu-rāta, who jumped aside and gave it a strong kick in the side with his heel. The boar quickly recovered itself while Viṣṇu-rāta taunted it and provoked it by throwing rocks. Then the big boar charged again. It had long, sharp tusks and stood about three feet high. The black bristles on its back were quivering and it snorted in anger. Viṣṇu-rāta knew that a boar can kill a man if it can gore him with his tusks. The danger quickened his reflexes. He let the boar get close and then leaped aside, driving his spear into the boar's head with all his strength. The animal was dead and the other boars fled.

He found a heavy branch and tied the boar's legs around it. Then he dragged it through the forest, back into the village. The sun was up now so Viṣṇu-rāta moved as quickly as possible. He didn't want his parents to see him. He dragged the boar into the courtyard of his father's house and shoved it into the doorway, his spear still buried in the boar's side. Then he started walking toward Prayāga.

4

I shall now describe the third meeting between Nārada-kṛpa Prabhu and Viṣṇu-rāta. I have heard all this personally from my *guru mahārāja.* He is the main participant in all these events, and the most reliable witness of his own internal and external activities. I am just trying to describe his life story for my own purification and for the pleasure of Vaiṣṇava friends who have asked that it be written.

After walking for an hour, he became exhausted and went to the Ganges to bathe. Only when he entered the water and saw some *sādhus* there praying, did Viṣṇu-rāta remember the chanting. Nārada-kṛpa had told him to chant, but he had forgotten that. He hadn't chanted at all during the whole violent incident the night before. "I am still a madman," he said to himself. But then he began to chant Hare Kṛṣṇa as he walked.

Viṣṇu-rāta entered the presence of his new friend, Nārada-kṛpa Prabhu. As soon as they exchanged greetings, Viṣṇu-rāta blurted out what had just happened. As he told it, he realized that he was as much to blame as his father.

"We are both madmen," said Viṣṇu-rāta. "But he has made me that way. I get angry and do things that I later regret. It's in our blood."

Nārada-kṛpa did not want to meddle in these family affairs or be disturbed by them. His spiritual master had told him to live simply and, "continuously chant the Hare Kṛṣṇa mantra," but what could he do? This young man was approaching him desperately, and he was interested in the message of Nārada Muni. He couldn't refuse him.

"A devotee should learn to control his anger," said Nārada-kṛpa. "If someone insults him, he should remain tolerant like a tree. He should just go on chanting."

"I didn't!" said Viṣṇu-rāta. "I forgot the chanting. Just when it would have helped. And I am ashamed to say it, but I killed another animal. My father called me a coward, so I wanted to prove to him . . . I killed a wild boar. We were both so angry that we could have killed each other!"

"There is always a reaction," said Nārada-kṛpa, "even for the killing of an ant."

"Can you tell me how I can be free of it? How did Nārada Muni convince you that it was wrong? How did he make you give it up once and for all?"

Nārada-kṛpa sighed as he remembered his spiritual master. Nārada Muni had told him to live alone with his wife and chant, but Viṣṇu-rāta's question drove him to remember Nārada. And to help a troubled soul who wanted to come to Kṛṣṇa consciousness—this would also please Nārada, the great preacher.

"I'll tell you what happened," said Nārada-kṛpa, "but listen well. Nārada saw me before I saw him. I was behind a tree taking aim at my next animal. I was having great luck that day. Within a short time I had shot a deer, a boar, and a rabbit. After making sure to shoot them somewhere that would not bring quick death, I rushed up and broke their legs. That is why Nārada noticed them, because they were still twisting in pain. O Viṣṇu-rāta, how horrible is the life of a cruel hunter! The sages say that he is so miserable, he shouldn't live and he shouldn't die."

"What can that mean?"

"I'll tell you. But it is not easy for me to speak of this again, even though it has been years since it happened. I normally don't talk of these things. I go on chanting and people can see my present example without need of explanation. But I must tell you because you are a hunter as I was, and I want to help you.

"Unfortunately, I caused even Nārada Muni pain in his heart because he saw my handiwork, the suffering animals. He thought, 'Who has committed this horrible crime?' He felt compassion for the animals because he sees all creatures as sons and daughters of Bhagavān Śrī Kṛṣṇa, the Supreme Father. He also knew that whoever had half-killed these creatures would be facing great suffering in his own life—he felt compassion for me. And there I was, hiding behind a tree. He was on his way to bathe in the sacred *tri-veṇī,* but instead of continuing on the path, he walked over to me. And as he did so, the animals I was stalking all ran away. When I saw what had happened, I became furious with him for causing such a disturbance."

"I know what that's like," smiled Viṣṇu-rāta. "When forest *sādhus* come tramping through the forest, my father curses them. 'Damn their lot!' he says, 'These fools are always getting in the way!' He curses them all the time and sometimes kicks them or throws rocks at them."

"Yes, yes," said Nārada-kṛpa, "I was so demoniac that I wanted to chastise even Nārada Muni. I looked up at him and started to form a curse, but then I couldn't. He immediately had a positive effect on me. You would have to see him to understand. I cannot explain it in words. Nārada was coming straight from the almighty Personality of Godhead. His body is effulgent. His movements are commanding, yet beautiful and gentle. He overpowered me, and suddenly I could do him no harm. I sensed that he was protected by a higher power.

"So I found myself speaking in a friendly, respectful way, something I never did. I addressed him, 'O *gosvāmī,* O great *sādhu!* Why have you walked off the path? I was just about to shoot several animals, but by your coming to me they have now fled.' He said, 'I have come to you to settle a doubt in my mind.' He asked me if I was the person who had half-killed so many animals. Of course I owned up to it. I didn't see anything wrong with it. I claimed them as mine. So Nārada said, 'Why didn't you kill them? Why did you leave them like that, twisting in pain?'"

"This practice of half-killing is wide-spread," said Viṣṇu-rāta.

"Yes, just as your father taught you this, my father taught me. I told Nārada Muni, 'When I see half-killed animals suffer, I feel great pleasure.' What an idiot I was—and a poor wretch—that I gloated as I told him. I wasn't angry with him, but I was just telling him how I felt about it.

"Nārada Muni is very powerful, Viṣṇu-rāta. He has cursed sinful persons for doing much less than I did. He once cursed two sons of demigods for being naked and drunk with women in an upper planet. Of course, his curse is also a form of blessing. But with me, he was very gentle. He was indirect at first. He said, 'I have one thing to ask of you.' I was not in the habit of giving alms. I am sure your father is the same way. Imagine, first a *sādhu* manages to chase away your prey by walking loudly on the path, and then he asks you for alms! But I was under Nārada's sweet control from the beginning. I really liked him! I thought, 'Let me give him whatever he wants.' I offered him skins. I wanted to take him to my home and let him take a pick of the best deer skin or tiger skin. Little did I know what he was actually begging for.

"Nārada Muni said, 'I don't want such things. But I beg you that from now on, you don't leave animals half-killed.' These words had a profound effect on me. Yet I couldn't figure out what he was saying. I knew that he was wonderful, but what a strange request! So I asked him, not as a challenge, but I just didn't know and I wanted him to tell me—'Please explain what is wrong with what I did to the animals?' It is only by his grace that I had reached this point of open-minded inquiry because usually, I didn't give a damn about *sādhus*. So Nārada replied that it was bad enough that I was killing at all, and for that I would have to suffer a reaction, 'But when you half-kill them, you give them great pain, and that same pain will be inflicted on you.'"

"This is the point I want to ask you about," said Viṣṇu-rāta. "I mean, did you change everything in your life—a complete turnabout—just by his uttering those few words? I ask because I am finding that the propensity to kill is deeply rooted in me. I have heard your words and they have changed my mind. But something goes deeper and I can't get rid of it yet."

"He convinced me by these words," said Nārada-kṛpa. "He said, 'All the animals that you have killed and given unnecessary pain to will kill you one after the other in your next life, and life after life.' But these weren't theoretical words. When he spoke them, I *saw* what he said. I saw myself being attacked by stags with antlers and tigers with teeth and claws. I saw myself and felt the pain coming, not just in one lifetime, but in hundreds of lives. I had killed hundreds and thousands of animals, and therefore each one . . . each one. I saw that it *would* happen. I was struck with fear!"*

"You saw a vision?"

"Call it what you like. As he uttered his words, I knew them as facts. I *felt* the nature of my own deeds. For the first time in my life, I realized that I wasn't going to get away with it. Every single act of pain I had caused others was going to come back to me. Each animal would have a chance to attack me, 'Remember me, Mṛgāri? I was the deer you left

---

* Nārada-kṛpa's elaboration of the "vision" of his future suffering revealed to him by Nārada, is very similar to an account which appears in the Fourth Canto of *Śrīmad-Bhāgavatam*. There, Nārada Muni stops King Prācīnabarhi from killing animals in sacrifice. The *Bhāgavatam* describes that by Nārada's influence, the king was able to see the animals in the sky and how they would kill him for his having killed them. The idea of the hunter hearing Nārada's words in a "vision" is not to be disregarded as something impossible, because we have the proof of *śāstra*. Nārada Muni is almost as good as the Supreme Personality of Godhead, and we have read in the *Caitanya-caritāmṛta* version of this history, that Nārada did other extraordinary feats, such as traveling from Vaikuṇṭha to Prayāga, and also restoring the half-killed animals to complete health:

> The three animals that were half-killed were then brought to their consciousness by the sage Nārada. Indeed, the animals got up and swiftly fled. When the hunter saw the half-killed animals flee, he was certainly struck with wonder.
>
> —*Cc. Madhya*, 24.263–4

—Vaiṣṇava-dāsānu dāsa

half-flapping by the river. Now I have come to get you.' 'Remember me, Mṛgāri? I was the rabbit . . . ' I knew that it was coming and I wanted to be spared. This was entirely due to Nārada's association. I was convinced on the spot that I was an offender. I fell down at his feet and asked how I could be saved."

Nārada-kṛpa was engrossed in the past. But then he suddenly returned to the present situation in the room, aware of Viṣṇu-rāta and the gravity of the moment.

"Now I see everything differently," said Nārada-kṛpa, "including the animals." While they spoke, little chipmunks ran in and out of the cottage, and sometimes birds perched on the window opening. Viṣṇu-rāta could see the harmony between man and beast that resulted from Nārada-kṛpa's nonviolence, and he felt a little envious.

"I have a way with animals too," said Viṣṇu-rāta. "I never developed it much, but if I want to, I can get really close to them and even talk to them."

Nārada-kṛpa smiled. "Then you should become their protector," he said.

Viṣṇu-rāta mulled those words over thoughtfully. He liked the idea.

"Did you have to do anything special to get rid of the sins?" Viṣṇu-rāta asked. "I mean, how did you know that you were forgiven? How do you know the reaction is gone?

"All I know," said Nārada-kṛpa, "is what my spiritual master, Nārada Muni, says. That may sound naive to some people, but I think you understand. And of course, I have my own feelings about it. But in *bhakti,* you don't have to perform separate atonement for sinful reactions. If you sincerely surrender to Kṛṣṇa and His representative, then Kṛṣṇa absolves you. He says in the *Bhagavad-gītā,* 'I will release you from the reaction to all your sins. Do not fear,' and He says to give up all other religious practices. If you just serve Kṛṣṇa by chanting and hearing as Nārada told me to do, then the slate is wiped clean. You can start new in this life."

"I think that's wonderful," said Viṣṇu-rāta. "I believe it. What else did Nārada teach you?"

"What else? Are you ready to hear for a hundred lifetimes? Nārada's teachings are comprehensive. I have been reading them in many scriptures, like *Śrīmad-Bhāgavatam* and *Rāmāyaṇa;* he is mentioned in practically all the scriptures. And he is still preaching wherever he goes. Sometimes he sits under a tree in a place like Lord Śiva's planet and hears from Lord Śiva or from Nāra-Nārāyaṇa Ṛṣi, and then goes somewhere else and explains what he has heard. When Nārada is there, the subject is always *bhakti-yoga.* Thank you for asking that question and reminding me of the glories of my spiritual master. Why don't we live near each other and spend our time speaking of what Nārada has said?"

"That would be wonderful," said Viṣṇu-rāta. "But can you tell me one thing about Nārada right now? What about his personal relationship with Lord Kṛṣṇa? Does he have one? Can you tell me about it?"

"Talking with you is exhilarating," said Nārada-kṛpa. "You ask good questions."

As with the previous meetings of Nārada-kṛpa and Viṣṇu-rāta, a few eager-to-hear villagers had gradually gathered in the room. Nārada-kṛpa's wife was also sitting just outside the door, listening. Nārada-kṛpa's friends and well-wishers were glad to see him enlivened by the enthusiastic visitor.

"Lord Kṛṣṇa expands into many Viṣṇu forms, which are all the Personality of Godhead," said Nārada-kṛpa. "He expands in the spiritual world in different Vaikuṇṭha planets for His pastimes with devotees who want to see Him in that form of opulence. Nārada Muni is particularly drawn to the opulence of Kṛṣṇa. But Nārada also knows that Kṛṣṇa in His original form, as the cowherd boy Govinda, is the topmost and sweetest form of the Supreme Lord. So when the Lord came in His original pastimes as a cowherd boy in the village of Vṛndāvana in Bharata-varśa, Nārada was also there. One time, Nārada came before Kṛṣṇa and began speaking His glories about the different pastimes Kṛṣṇa had performed in Vṛndāvana, and then Nārada began to predict with exact accuracy the future pastimes that the Lord would perform in Vṛndāvana, in Mathurā, and in Dvārakā. Nārada can see the future and he enthusiastically glorified Kṛṣṇa. Another time, Nārada Muni came to see Kṛṣṇa in Dvārakā, and Kṛṣṇa got off His throne and bowed down to him. Nārada said, 'You may do this if You like because You like to honor *brāhmaṇas*, but actually I am just Your eternal servant. My prayer is to serve You eternally with love.' So Nārada and Kṛṣṇa have a very intimate relationship, one that is based on devotional service. Nārada Muni is a preacher. He travels to all the different planets of the material worlds and the spiritual worlds, playing his *vīṇā* while singing *bhajanas*. Sometimes he tells humorous stories to preach pure philosophy.

"He is the most compassionate. He has become the guru of even exalted Vaiṣṇavas like Dhruva Mahārāja, who in the beginning had material desires. And he is the guru of Prahlāda Mahārāja. Prahlāda said, 'I was falling into the way of the demons as if into a pit of snakes, but my spiritual master, Nārada saved me. How could I ever forget him?' Nārada is very liberal. It's not that he only goes to the aristocratic persons or the demigods, but he tries to spread the Lord's mercy even to persons who are completely covered over and encrusted with sinful activities . . ."

When he came to these words, Nārada-kṛpa stopped and tears began to roll out of his eyes. To those present, he seemed to fall into a trance, absorbed in the "other world" of remembrance of Nārada, with whom he had had personal *darśana*. After about five minutes, Nārada-kṛpa returned to external consciousness.

"Why don't we have *kīrtana?*" he asked.

Viṣṇu-rāta asked Nārada-kṛpa for permission to build a cottage nearby and stay there and chant Hare Kṛṣṇa. Nārada-kṛpa agreed. But then Viṣṇu-rāta became doubtful. "Maybe I should go back for awhile first," he said, "but for tonight, can I sleep in your yard?"

During the night, Viṣṇu-rāta had an unusual dream. It featured animals who were living in the forest near his hometown. They were talking with one another. They were all terrified that Viṣṇu-rāta and his father, Paśu, were coming to kill them. "They call *us* ferocious," said a wild boar. "but that boy is ferocious. He has a killer's instinct. I am afraid that he will kill the whole pack."

"Why do they do it? Why do they kill?" asked a baby boar.

"Because they are humans, that's why," said a lone male boar. "Humans kill animals. That's all."

"Where can we hide?" asked a rabbit.

"Can't we get together and attack them?" asked a buck with big antlers.

"No, we can't get together, as you well know," replied another big animal, "and we're all afraid of the tigers."

"Even if we could get together," said a tiger, who appeared in their midst in a temporarily friendly mood, "they are too intelligent, devilishly intelligent, and they have iron weapons."

"But I heard that Viṣṇu-rāta has stopped killing," said a bright green parrot.

"Maybe it's true, but I wouldn't trust him," said a snake coiling down a tree branch.

"And even if one Viṣṇu-rāta does stop killing, what difference will it make?" said a spider dangling in mid-air. "His father is more fierce, and he is angrier than ever."

"We need a protector, we need a protector," said several animals together.

Viṣṇu-rāta awoke and thought at once of Nārada-kṛpa's words, "So you should become their protector." He sat up and looked around. He was in the smooth earthen clearing around Nārada-kṛpa's cottage. He could tell from the stars and moon that it was about midnight. Viṣṇu-rāta took the dream seriously and tried to think what it meant. "The animals need a protector," he thought, "and I am their protector." He thought of waiting until the morning and asking Nārada-kṛpa if this interpretation of the dream was correct. If he got his permission, Viṣṇu-rāta decided that he would make a campaign against hunters and protect animals. He would be the perfect one to do it. He could fight and he could travel in the forest. He could get close to animals. He knew all the ins and outs of hunting and could spoil all the attempts at hunting by the rascals and demons. Even his own father wouldn't be able to hunt because Viṣṇu-rāta would sabotage his attempts. He would protect the animals.

Viṣṇu-rāta decided not to wait and ask permission from Nārada-kṛpa. If Viṣṇu-rāta's father found out that the sage had advised such a plan, he might come there with other hunters and harm Nārada-kṛpa. Besides, Viṣṇu-rāta thought, this was his own idea, his own dream. It was something that he had to personally do, regardless of what other persons thought or said. Maybe this was how God was talking to him. This would be *his* contribution. He would protect the animals.

Although part of him sensed that he was being impetuous, Viṣṇu-rāta decided to start at once for his hometown. He washed his face in the nearby river, made obeisances before the *tulasī* plant, and said "Hare Kṛṣṇa." Then he started out quickly on his mission. He began to run and his mind ran also, sketching out plans for action. He had no time for chanting Hare Kṛṣṇa now. He had work to do.

5

All glories to Nārada Muni who is a *śaktyāveśa-avatāra* of Lord Kṛṣṇa, appearing throughout the three worlds just to teach the ways of pure devotional service. As Lord Kṛṣṇa states in the *Bhagavad-gītā*, "Of the sages among the demigods, I am Nārada." It is further proclaimed in the *Skanda Purāṇa*, in the words of Parvata Muni, "My dear friend Nārada Muni, you are glorified as the sage among the demigods. By your mercy, even a lowborn person like this hunter can immediately become attached to Lord Kṛṣṇa."

Glories to all the devotees appearing in the line of Nārada Muni's disciplic succession. Nārada's direct disciple is Śrīla Vyāsadeva, who compiled all the Vedic Sanskrit literatures. Vyāsa's disciple and son is Śukadeva Gosvāmī, who spoke *Śrīmad-Bhāgavatam* and made it sweeter by his own eloquence and realization. Therefore, the *Śrīmad-*

Bhāgavatam is flowing from the original directions given by Nārada Muni to Vyāsa.

I am an obscure spirit soul who has wandered into this material world because of many wrong desires. I have no right or qualification to praise the great sages, but my spiritual master has ordered me to do so, provided I adhere strictly to the Vaiṣṇava *paramparā,* and behave according to the rules and regulations. I am happy to be able to compose *Viṣṇu-rāta Vijaya,* but I ask my readers to forgive me for the crudeness of its presentation. My purpose will be fulfilled if the readers will reflect on the great mercy which is available in Vaiṣṇava association. May everyone become happy and fulfilled by gaining service to the lotus feet of the Vaiṣṇavas even in this lifetime.

Now I will tell what happened when Viṣṇu-rāta returned to his home village with a plan to become the protector of the animals.

He figured it all out while walking from Prayāga to his home. Viṣṇu-rāta knew those forests and jungles like the back of his hand. There was a hidden cave on a hilltop, and he would make that his residence and headquarters for his campaign. He would protect the wildlife by directly interfering with all hunters. He would blow a conch shell to warn the animals. His woodcraft was far superior to that of most of the hunters in the area, so he could easily conceal himself from them, while at the same time stalking them. Whenever they got near a group of animals, he would sound his horn and they would lose their catch. He also planned to actually confront some of the hunters and preach to them. Viṣṇu-rāta expected that it would be risky work. He would have to be ready to die if necessary, to throw himself between an arrow and an animal, but by these efforts, he would eventually convince the hunters of their sinfulness, or drive them away in frustration. If they did manage to kill an animal, then he would raid the village at night and slice up the skins. He could hide in the cave, which he would cover over with bushes and twigs.

He imagined a band of frustrated hunters calling him out of hiding to discuss his intentions. They would be very angry at first, but gradually they would be moved by his arguments, by his very presence, just as he had been moved by the association of Nārada-kṛpa Prabhu. Gradually they would give up their arguments and be converted to nonviolence. He pictured them all breaking their bows and vowing never to kill again. And among the converts would be his father. They would embrace, and Paśu would apologize to him. He would admit his own mistake in attacking his father the way he had. Maybe they would all go to Nārada-kṛpa together, he leading them in triumph. Nārada-kṛpa would praise him for his quick and thorough success and everyone would be pleased with him.

But although Viṣṇu-rāta had his plans for victory, the war against the hunters lasted only one day. The first hunter to come out was a young man, who was not as experienced as Viṣṇu-rāta. Viṣṇu-rāta was able to stalk rings around him, and it went

well. Without even knowing what happened, the hunter heard low blasts of a conch and wasn't able to find any game. He went home baffled, and told the village elders about the strange sound.

There were about a dozen full-time hunters in that area, and many sportsmen who liked to try their luck from time to time. Viṣṇu-rāta duped them all. They couldn't even see him, but some of them shouted, "Whoever you are, you'd better stop this! If we catch hold of you, we'll break your neck."

Then Viṣṇu-rāta saw Ambulal, the son of the utensil maker who had traveled with him the first time they went to see Nārada-kṛpa Prabhu. He was out with a few other boys for some afternoon rabbit-shooting. Viṣṇu-rāta leaped out of the woods and confronted them.

Don't kill the animals," said Viṣṇu-rāta, and he spread out his arms as if to defend the whole forest behind him.

"Viṣṇu-rāta!" exclaimed Ambulal. "So it's you who's blowing the conch."

"You should know better," said Viṣṇu-rāta. "You remember what we heard from that sage in Prayāga?"

"I remember," said his friend, "but since then I've discussed it with my teachers. They say that God has arranged it this way. One living being is food for another. Even the vegetarian kills to eat. The grass is alive, isn't it? What are wheat or vegetables but living plants? So what's the difference?"

Viṣṇu-rāta was suddenly perplexed. He had never thought about it that way before. But still, that didn't justify killing animals.

"I don't know all the answers," said Viṣṇu-rāta, "but I've come to protect the animals. So you might as well go home because I won't let you kill them." He then ran off out of sight into the woods. After a few attempts to continue their hunting, the boys went home, followed by the loud blasts of Viṣṇu-rāta's hidden conch. Since the conch blowing was working well but his preaching was inadequate, he decided to concentrate on remaining hidden. But now his identity was known, as the boys spread it around the village.

In mid-afternoon, a group of four full-time hunters came out together, shouting his name. "Viṣṇu-rāta! We've come to get you! Turn yourself in or we'll shoot you."

Viṣṇu-rāta became himself a hunted animal. But as he was expert in stalking animals, he was also expert in the role of the hunted. He kept out of their reach, and only once or twice did they even catch a glimpse of him. At first he didn't think they were actually serious about shooting him, but then an arrow whizzed past him and stuck in a tree. He was frightened but excited by the challenge, and he became even more determined to outwit them. He increased his distance from the hunters so that he was beyond their reach, yet his conch blowing still kept all the animals fleeing in a wide radius. The group of four hunters went home, cursing loudly.

In the late afternoon, when most hunters had given up, Viṣṇu-rāta heard the steps of a single hunter. He positioned himself on the promontory of a hill, and looking into the valley, he saw that the lone hunter was his father. When his father took aim at a deer, Viṣṇu-rāta blew the conch and the animal ran away. Then his father began to shout loudly into the forest.

"Viṣṇu-rāta! I know you're out there . . . listen to me for your own good . . . You ain't no son of mine . . . but your mother . . . she doesn't wanna see you dead . . . me neither . . . but if you don't get outta here . . . you're gonna be in serious trouble . . . the men is formin' a big party . . . they're gonna come for you . . . we ain't foolin' around . . . I'll probably be with 'em myself . . . But I'm just comin' out now for your mother . . . be warned!"

Viṣṇu-rāta felt mixed emotions as he heard the angry shouts but thought of his soft-hearted mother. He felt pity for his father as he saw him crashing through the undergrowth, carrying his bow and arrows. Little did his father know that those bow and arrows were sending him to hell by his own bad karma.

Viṣṇu-rāta continued to stalk his father from a distance. Near the edge of the forest, his father spied several large wild turkeys on the ground by a tree. He crouched quietly and slowly fixed an arrow to his bow. But just as he pointed it upwards, the unseen conch blasted out with many quick notes. The birds were startled and scattered unharmed.

Then the protector of the animals returned home to his cave, just as the night was darkening, in a hunter-free forest. Viṣṇu-rāta made a small smokeless fire in the cave to warm his hands, and he ate a meal of berries and bread he had carried from Prayāga. He wished the animals could somehow be grateful for his protection, but he didn't really expect them to reciprocate. Maybe eventually he would be able to communicate more with them and they could express their thanks. While he was thinking like this, he heard a rattlesnake moving in a corner of the cave. Viṣṇu-rāta caught it on a stick and threw it outside. He laughed to himself as he did it. But then as he went to sleep by his little campfire he thought, "All the animals know that man is their enemy, but *I* don't have to be their enemy. And now I have become the enemy of the hunters. But actually I am their friend . . . I have to save them from their karma . . . but I don't know all the answers . . . I have to learn . . . I am no Nārada Muni."

Viṣṇu-rāta woke while the sun was rising. The first thing he saw was the village policeman sitting at the entrance of the cave.

"Good morning," said the policeman in a relaxed voice. He was sitting in the half lotus position, which comes naturally to all people in Bharatavarśa.

"How did you find me here?" asked Viṣṇu-rāta, a note of irritation in his voice. It was acutely disappointing to have been discovered so quickly

and so easily, and he felt a twinge of anger at this intruder.

"You're not the only stalker in the world," said the policeman.

Viṣṇu-rāta was wary. The policeman was a friend, but after all, he had the power to arrest him. Viṣṇu-rāta was also cold and hungry. He felt trapped in the cave, and he tried to recall the layout of the area and plan his escape.

"I've come to warn you," said the policeman, "that all the hunters and many others are coming today to get you. You got away yesterday, but they are going to comb the whole forest until they find you. They are really riled up."

"But am I wrong?" Viṣṇu-rāta challenged. He thought this policeman was someone who might understand. "Is it right that they torture and kill the animals? They don't know about the karma, but it's a fact. For all that killing, they will have to suffer reaction. Do you know about karma?"

Viṣṇu-rāta shivered. The policeman threw over the extra *cādar* he had brought for Viṣṇu-rāta. He mumbled his thanks and threw it over his shoulders.

"Yes, I know about karma," said the policeman. "I learned it from my mother and grandmother. I believe it. But you cannot force people to change their karma."

"But *you* force people," said Viṣṇu-rāta. "Haven't you come here to force me?"

"No, I haven't come for that," said the policeman. "Yes, I force people to obey man's laws, but God's law is voluntary."

Viṣṇu-rāta recalled that he had promised himself not to get into debates, but this was a different situation. This was a sincere conversation—he had to say what he felt.

"God's law may be voluntary," said Viṣṇu-rāta, "but still, if you don't obey it, you will be punished. God allows you to kill because you have free will, but nevertheless, you will be punished for it."

"I see you have become a philosopher," said the policeman, smiling. "*Sādhus* like you teach us and set the example. *Sādhus* stop their own bad karma, and tell everyone how to stop theirs—by preaching. But even *sādhus* have to behave peacefully. There are laws that everyone has to obey."

"But what if man's laws are against God's laws?"

"In that case, I have to enforce man's laws," said the policeman, and he sucked in his lips. "The world is not a place of perfect justice, but as I told you last time, even if there is some imperfection, we have to do our duty. Everyone works in their *varṇa* and we pray to God to purify us. The *sādhus* especially can do that in society. But not what *you're* doing—interfering with hunters and destroying property. One boy said you even knocked him down. For myself, I am not so sure that hunting is against God's law, but if you think it is, then you should become a nonviolent *sādhu.*"

"I will," said Viṣṇu-rāta.

"I think you should," said the policeman. "I admire you for it. I'm saying this confidentially because your father might not like to hear me say it, but I admire that you have been going to hear from Nārada-kṛpa and that you are able to assimilate those pure teachings. It is wonderful that you want to practice nonviolence and to love God. In my opinion, you will have to move to another province in order to do this. It is not fair to your parents to launch your attack right here. Maybe in the future, they can be proud of you if you become a truly peaceful and saintly person. But don't harass them like this."

"I don't mean to harass them, it's just that . . . "

"If you stay here, there will be violence," said the policeman, "and before I let that happen, I will have to arrest you. But I haven't come to do that. I came to wish you well, so I am leaving now." The policeman left the cave and started down the steep embankment.

Viṣṇu-rāta called after him, "Thanks for the *cādar.*" The policeman waved without looking back.

6

Viṣṇu-rāta left the familiar forest of his home and again journeyed to Prayāga. He surrendered himself as a fool before his spiritual master and asked to be accepted as a disciple. Nārada-kṛpa accepted him and ordered him to take up the life which Nārada had advised, of continuously chanting Hare Kṛṣṇa and worshiping Tulasī. Viṣṇu-rāta happily obeyed.

Thus began his long apprenticeship of living with his spiritual master. In methodical order, he studied under Nārada-kṛpa the teachings of Nārada Muni, *Śrīmad-Bhāgavatam*, and all other important Vaiṣṇava literatures. He also learned to become peaceful and to chant. Sometimes Viṣṇu-rāta had nightmares in which animals came to attack him, but his spiritual master told him not to be afraid of them. Viṣṇu-rāta never returned home, but he occasionally received news. Hunting resumed there as usual, but apparently some of the young men had found other professions, and others ceased the practice of leaving the animals half-dead. Paśu was gloomy and angry for a while, but even he—to everyone's surprise—stopped half-killing animals. He was quoted as saying, "What my son said is crazy, but I don't break their legs no more. Maybe it ain't necessary."

One time, Ambulal visited Prayāga. He brought some *capātīs* from Viṣṇu-rāta's mother. In return, Viṣṇu-rāta sent some *tulasī* leaves to his mother. And this time, Viṣṇu-rāta was able to answer his friend's questions about karma and the effects of meat-eating.

I have told Viṣṇu-rāta's story thus far based on his own talks and as we have heard from reliable witnesses. He is very humble, and will not allow us to tell the details of his many wonderful activities in his later years. He said, "If you want to write 'my life,' the only thing worth describing is how I was saved by Nārada-kṛpa Prabhu. Tell how I gave up my ways as a hunter." And so we are complying for the time being. We will end our story somewhat prematurely. But the fact is, there are many glorious events in Viṣṇu-rāta's life *after* he gave up his life as a hunter. At least let me tell of them in code form.

Viṣṇu-rāta Mahārāja traveled widely throughout Bharata-varśa, preaching the message of *bhagavata-dharma*. Many people heard from him, and thus, in his own way, he served as a *sparśa-maṇi*, or touchstone from Nārada Muni's disciplic succession. As stated by Lord Kṛṣṇa in the *Bhagavad-gītā,* whoever speaks the message of *bhakti-yoga* becomes the dearmost servant of the Lord.

Viṣṇu-rāta Swami often told audiences of his former life, and advised everyone to give up all kinds of animal slaughter and animal cruelty. Otherwise, one has to face horrible karmic reactions during many future lives. As a result of these strong speeches, one landowner gave Viṣṇu-rāta Mahārāja a donation for a cow protection farm and animal sanctuary in a large tract of land. This project still continues after many years.

Under the direction of his spiritual master, Viṣṇu-rāta Swami also wrote commentaries to scriptures as well as some original works,* and he wrote some scrolls on topics such as chanting the holy names, the worship of Tulasī, and the benefits of hearing the pastimes of Kṛṣṇa that were passed from person to person. Although he never again tried to accost hunters in the woods by blowing a conch or destroying their skins, he continued to oppose hunting and animal slaughter, and thus he wrote a scroll denouncing it on scriptural grounds in the aboriginal language of the hunters. Viṣṇu-rāta Swami and his associates copied and distributed these scrolls widely, and there are many instances in which people gave up their practices of killing or leaving animals half-dead, as a direct

---

* One of these is included as an appendix to this book. (Vaiṣṇava-dāsānu dāsa)

result of hearing his writings, or by being won over by him in a face-to-face debate.

This biographical data must unfortunately remain sketchy, but I would like to add my personal appreciation for the influence of Viṣṇu-rāta Swami in my own life. When I met him, I was indulging in all the four main sinful activities: illicit sex, intoxication, meat-eating, and gambling. He opened my eyes to the fact that I was completely wasting the rare opportunity granted by human life, which is meant for attaining self-realization and devotional service to Lord Kṛṣṇa. He effectively put me on the path of *bhakti-yoga,* from which I pray never to depart. He did this not only by repeating the words of *śāstra*—something he did faithfully—but by taking the time to guide me with his personal concern. His own example of simplicity and honesty in spiritual life—not pretending to be something greater than others, and never abusing the charity of the public, while always strictly following the vows of *sannyāsa*—continues to be the most powerful, motivating influence in my life.

Viṣṇu-rāta Swami has not broken the world's record for the most disciples ever initiated, neither has he opened more temples than any other *ācārya,* but I don't think spiritual advancement can always be measured in those terms. He spoke of himself as an ex-hunter who was still struggling with bad dreams and who had no deep taste for the holy names (although he chanted sixty-four rounds daily without fail), but even his so-called limitations are appealing to me, and they enforce my own commitments. I do not see his confession of struggle as a disqualification, but rather, it puts the *reality* of spiritual life straight in front of my eyes, giving me constant encouragement in my own stubborn case. By his example, he convinces me to never give up devotional service, even when I fail after many attempts to chant with love and to realize that I should completely dedicate my body, mind and words in the service of Kṛṣṇa. I fall repeatedly on the path, but Viṣṇu-rāta Swami is always there, gently smiling and encouraging me by saying, "You are doing nicely, Prabhu. Kṛṣṇa appreciates your sincerity. Keep trying; you have nothing to lose and the gain is very great."

Viṣṇu-rāta Swami says that the only thing in his life that is worth mentioning is that he met his spiritual master. Meeting the spiritual master is certainly the most significant event that has occurred in *my* life, which was otherwise doomed. And even His Grace Nārada-kṛpa Prabhu told of a similar event in his own life. So let it be as Viṣṇu-rāta Swami wishes, that he can be remembered solely by the fact that he was a hunter and was rescued by Nārada Muni's direct servant. I will not disobey his request by describing his life in more detail. I am satisfied to remember him traveling to Prayāga and inquiring sincerely from Nārada-kṛpa Prabhu, abandoning his family and occupation, and surrendering at a young age to the life of full-time devotional service. I am sufficiently enlivened to have told this much of his life, provided it be received with appreciation by readers who are hankering for accounts of real people in Kṛṣṇa consciousness. The story of Viṣṇu-rāta is certainly true, and it is a solid instance of the good effect of Vaiṣṇava association.

May the Supreme Lord Śrī Kṛṣṇa continue to grant us His compassion—which the Personified *Vedas* state is the most glorious of *all* the inconceivable qualities of the Lord—by sending the Vaiṣṇava *ācāryas* and their representatives into all the dark corners of this material world. Without the example and preaching of the Lord's devotees, the world would be plunged into the complete hopelessness of *tamo-* and *rajo-guṇa,* without a chance of rescue from the torments of repeated birth and death. This is confirmed in the Vedic scriptures: "According to their karma, all living entities are wandering throughout the entire universe. Some of them are being elevated to the upper planetary systems, and some are going down to the lower planetary systems. Out of many millions of wandering living entities, one who is very fortunate gets an opportunity to associate with a bona fide spiritual master by the grace of Kṛṣṇa. By the mercy of both Kṛṣṇa and the spiritual master, such a person receives the seed of *bhakti,* of devotional service."

Bowing at your feet, I close this story. May Nārada Muni always be happy with you.

nārada-muni, bajāya vīṇā,
'rādhikā-ramaṇa'-nāme

The great soul, Nārada Muni plays a *vīṇā,* vibrating the sound, 'Rādhikā-ramaṇa,' O Kṛṣṇa, attractor of Śrīmatī Rādhikā . . .

Notes

The anonymous biographer of *Viṣṇu-rāta Vijaya* claims that Viṣṇu-rāta Swami composed various writings. But only one manuscript, an original work, has survived. We have already been informed that Viṣṇu-rāta sometimes had dreams of his former life as a hunter, so it comes as no surprise that he has written about it. These vignettes may be actual dreams that he witnessed, or fictional devices used to bring out preaching points on his favorite theme of nonviolence to animals and the need for Kṛṣṇa consciousness. The manuscript is written in his aboriginal language, from the same period and style as the biography. We have rendered it freely into modern English for contemporary readers.

—Vaiṣṇava-dāsānu dāsa

Dreams of an Ex-Hunter
(by Viṣṇu-rāta Swami)

I am being cut to pieces. A lion is chasing me. I am trying to save my father. We are all being dragged down a rapids over a falls, into a pit of fire and snakes . . .

Walking down a road. Birds are singing. It's delightful. Just before dawn, the forest emerging, the road becoming visible, but not quite yet. Here alone, joy leaps in my chest. I am talking aloud to my spiritual master who is not here physically, but who once was, and who is again in my memory of him. The birds, the light increasing, the ability to walk well, if even for a little while longer, and being thankful to have a mind and to be sheltered in *bhakti-yoga.* Life like this! O dreams, you cannot equal this waking reality! Or am I dreaming again?

That *sādhu* I saw when I was a young child. He is giving me a sweet again. "Nice boy, don't tell your father." White-haired, thin-muscled *sādhu* in the forest lean-to. Father kicked your *śalagrama-śila!* Please forgive us. I did not know. Please forgive my father, we did not know. Mother served me cow's meat. We did not know . . .

But ignorance is no excuse.
But ignorance is no excuse.

Father enters the room with a ball of fur. We eat it. Our teeth spring out like fangs. We turn into pointy-eared demons, afraid yet laughing.

"Viṣṇu-rāta! Get up! Get up!"

"Fiercy is his name," said a disembodied spirit.

"No, he's Viṣṇu-rāta now, as named by his *guru mahārāja*."

"Call him any name you like, we've got his number. He's the one who killed the deer. He's the one who killed the birds. He's the one who left them broken-legged. And now we've come to give him his!"

"No, he's Viṣṇu-rāta."

"No, he's Fiercy."

"Wake up, Viṣṇu-rāta, there is nothing to fear. Why don't you remember to chant the holy names? Throw off that old coil and take the names, *now* before it's too late."

Hare Kṛṣṇa Hare Kṛṣṇa Kṛṣṇa Kṛṣṇa Hare Hare/Hare Rāma Hare Rāma Rāma Rāma Hare Hare.

This is only a dream. This is only a reality. I killed many animals and they came back. And in the next life I come back.

Sleeping under the stars. Preaching to an audience on Kṛṣṇa consciousness. My father and mother enter the outer ring of the audience. "And here is an example of a hunter," I say. Father shoots an arrow at my heart. My heart flies out of my body to protect me. My spiritual master should be protected. O policeman, here is your *cādar* back. Hanging on a tree, a man dangling. Don't think it won't happen to you.

"Where are these voices coming from?"

On a deathbed. I am sorry. Please forgive me. It's too late. No. Tell them to go away and bring near my loving friends. Please, I don't want to see the animal faces at my bedside. Tell them to go away. Why do the humans seem to have animal faces? Why does the policeman have an elephant head? Why is the doctor an elk? Did I ever kill him? I didn't want to harm people. We were *good* hunters, not murderers. We were a good family. She was a chaste wife, he was a father, I was a meat-chewing son.

Vālmikī enters. "Yes," he said, "you read it right. The murderer and the hunter are much the same. Your mother told it wrong."

Why has the man got the head of a stork? Does this mean in my next life and the life after that we will have these bodies?

"O Fiercy-rata, it means what it means."

"Give your feet to the diners, they will like to eat them."

"I'll have his white meat, please."

"I'll take a piece of liver. And cook it well. Pluck it out fresh please."

"Chopped toes for me."

"His eyeball in soup, if you don't mind, and hurry, we're not feeling well."

"Serve us a Fiercy-rāta, please."

"And a napkin. Bring out the hunters to dance for us. Let's have a dinner that is unforgettable. Let's have fun with his body."

I dreamt a bow was being broken. It was my father's bow. It was my bow. Nārada Muni was laughing and Mṛgāri was breaking the bows, only he was not Mṛgāri anymore, but a self-effulgent devotee chanting peacefully in his cottage, and as he chanted, the bows broke. There was a rainbow across the sky, and the arrows were flowers and the animals were happy to hear to the bows breaking. I woke up saying, "It's the Revolution at last, the breaking of the bows."

The sages were on the march. The streams were running freely down the mountainsides. Foxes stopped to drink the clear water, and fawns and calves stopped to drink, and the foxes did not attack them. The tigers were fed by the sages who were on the march. They were walking together singing *harināma,* carrying *daṇḍas;* people gave them garlands, and more sages came out from hiding and joined them. Their numbers swelled and farmers and children joined them in a *mahā-harināma.* Even the animals ran alongside, chanting in their own way.

I was dreaming and I thought, "This cannot be." But Nārada-kṛpa Prabhu came to me saying, "In God's kingdom it is possible. It is like this in His abode."

"But when are the hunters coming?" I asked. "Give me my conch shell and a knife and I will stop them."

"Here they cannot come," said a voice from the mountains. "Those who come here are safe. Even ex-hunters may come here when they give up their ways."

"Am *I* here or am I dreaming it only?"

"You are here if you want to be. You must strongly want to be here. When you are awake you must work for this."

"Tell me how."

"Think of Me, become My devotee, worship Me, and work for Me here by telling everyone you meet about Me, Lord Kṛṣṇa. Then you will come to Me without doubt."

My dreams have improved, but I still have nightmares sometimes. Funny, you think you've attained the spiritual world by one happy vision, but there is still more attachment to the old ties. Still more visitations from those to whom you were cruel.

I was in a big hall. It was cold. I wanted someone to come and put a blanket on me, but I couldn't ask. I bellowed. They came and fed me. But they left me in the dark. Many black flies tormented my nose.

I was a dog, whining; I was a cat, killed.

I was a cow of the *sādhus* at an *āśrama.* Bony haunches, shivering to get rid of the flies, but you can't shake them off your nose. Whisk them with your tail if you can. The old man is poor. He lets you out the door. You wander down the streets. Look out for the vicious dogs who bare their teeth and yelp. If they get too bad, charge them with your horns. Many people respect cows and pet you.

I pass urine and a man in the village, a passerby, runs to collect it before it splashes to the ground. But if I try to eat a cabbage from the vendor's stand, "Ho! Hut!" He beats my back with a big stick. I clatter down the street. What good is it to be a holy cow in a holy town if you cannot eat? Rags and paper in the gutter. Chew anything.

If it could only stop. I once had so much time and wasted it. Now if I could just understand and be warm in a place with a spiritual guide.

How long will I go on sliding down through the species? I want to apologize to someone and ask for release. But it doesn't seem possible. Just keep in mind that if you ever get a chance as a human . . . But it's so hard—it only happens once in a million lifetimes and then you forget. The others influence you. You get a big tongue and belly and genitals. Women in the fire light. The urgency in your loins. I must remember to learn how to live and see a way out. Oh, how my head aches and arms ache and legs ache, the eating out of my innards, the cruelty and fear . . . I am simply lost in a black hole with everyone else here. Where is my friend, someone to meet me in a warm place and speak kind words? Where is there *not* fear? Where is peace? Where is happiness? A place in the sun?

My spiritual master comes to me in a disguised form. I wake from myriad dreams and can hardly remember a single image. The dreams of an ex-hunter. Better not to sleep then. Stay awake all night and no daytime snoozes either—late morning sex fantasies if I sleep. But who can keep such a vigil on his soul? Only recently have I been good. Mostly my heart is swarming with old deeds and unspent material desires—to eat, to mate—and I'm afraid even now of what may happen to my body and mind. What if I am captured and taken away from my peaceful cottage? O spiritual master, make me bold like you and dependent on Kṛṣṇa. I don't know Kṛṣṇa, but I know you.

Why don't I engage myself fully in your service? Let it be, let it be.

How can I keep a constant vigil? You have given me the task of chanting the holy names. I say, "the task." Just see my mentality. I am surrendered to you only in surface ways. You know my heart is still tied to this mind from many lifetimes. I am only pretending to be a *sādhu,* chanting and speaking holy discourses. I am hungry just like the cows at lunchtime. I refrain from sex with my genitals, but not in my mind. I once defied my hunter-father, but have never developed compassion for the likes of him. I sit here, complacent and smug, thinking that I have saved myself and that I am better than others. I can't cry out to Kṛṣṇa with any feeling. I feel only sorrow for myself and . . . I am afraid to sleep because then the dreams come—and the animals I killed. So I sit up at night, and people say, "He's so holy, he stays up at night calling in love to the Omnipotent God whom he loves like a lover." They do not know that I am empty.

But you, my spiritual master, know all these things. I have faith in your words and in the cleansing power of the *bhakti-yoga* duties you have given me. I do not mean to complain, but this is the truth—I have no devotion, only a tiny fraction of a moment have I been good, and behind me swarms a seemingly infinite past of cruelty and horror in individual lives. In the future, who can say? Give me trust and faith. Let me at least end this lifetime without giving up the order that you have given me. And wherever I must go in my next life, let me remember Kṛṣṇa's names.

They asked me have I ever dreamt of Kṛṣṇa. Do I? Do I dream of His abode? I must say, "No, not yet." I wouldn't dare, I think. How can one who mostly dreams of the filth and sweat and fantasies of fear—*sometimes* dream of the all-pure one? It's not fitting.

Does it mean I have to first empty all this filth? But it's like chasing away a million flies in the summertime. There are too many. Once I began the wrong way, I fell down endlessly, and it's all retained in my unconscious memory. Enough. I won't speak deliberately of it and waste my time. But no, I don't dream of the Lord because I am not fit.

But sometimes as I clench my *japa* beads during the night—in the midst of a bad dream—I feel the knots of wood in my hand and I think, "These are my beads to chant to Kṛṣṇa if I can." I know there are devotees who see Him in dreams. At least He is enabling me to *cast off the worst dreams when they come.* And when I awake, there is no dream but actual Kṛṣṇa conscious duties to perform. "Get up, Viṣṇu-rāta, go bathe in the sacred river." Your name is Viṣṇu-rāta dāsa, and you are living in a sacred place near a sacred river. Take to the holy names, you are allowed to chant them and keep under their protection. I may not dream of Kṛṣṇa, but I am awake, and that is more important. I beg the Lord, please don't let me fall down. Please forgive me.

Little has changed since I last went to sleep and dreamt: the hunters are still killing. But I will speak the truth. For every hair on the body of the cow the farmers kill (and they don't even have to hunt them), the farmer will have to rot in a hell for a thousand years! For every single cow killed. I didn't dream it: it's the law. Do you believe me, or do you want to wait and see?

"O hypocrite preacher, you used to do it yourself."

"But I've stopped. He stopped me. Now I don't kill even the ants. See them in the light on the ground? They have the right to live, that's all. Kṛṣṇa is not pleased if you kill His less intelligent sons or unpretty daughters. He is maintaining them and you have no right to kill them."

"Preacher, speak till you are blue in the face if it eases your own guilt, you superstitious dolt. We will kill as we like and eat 'em. You and 'God' can't do a thing."

"I don't speak for you. You are too far gone. You have to wait for death. But some will learn sense, as did Mṛgāri, feeling the truth in his bones—that you cannot escape the law of a life for a life; everything comes back. You may listen or not, but we are speaking."

Here ends the Dreams of an Ex-Hunter. *What follows, is a fragment of a scroll written by Viṣṇu-rāta Swami called, "A Statement by An Ex-Hunter." We have included it here to complete the record—Vaiṣṇava-dāsānu dāsa*

Dear Friends, May this fortunate ex-hunter speak a few words to you?

Please spare the animals' pain, for your sake and theirs. Excuse me, but you have come to a wrong conclusion if you think that this killing of God's creatures can go on without the killers suffering by retaliation. Please consider it. I do not wish to disturb anyone. It is a fact that I come from an angry race and I myself tend to be angry. But now I am at peace. I do not wish to blow my conch shell to spoil your savagery or to destroy your honest livelihood. Yet what kind of a life is it that takes pleasure in others' dying? The cow, deer, rabbit, birds, and even the fish are *people,* although not as intelligent as you or I.

We enjoy the sunshine, a nice meal, a refreshing drink, the touch of our beloved mate, a romp through the fields when we are young, and so do these animals. (How derisively we call them "animals," but we too have their basic traits of eating, mating, sleeping and defending. We humans are also animals, but at the same time, we are human beings, supposedly higher creatures. Where is our compassion?)

The killing is not necessary. We have been conditioned to think that we need animal flesh in order to be strong and to be healthy. We have come to relish it. But we do not need it. The gourmet can feast on meals made from grains, milk, vegetables, fruits, all cooked and spiced and fully satisfying. Please consider it. Join us, who have given up this ghastly business of animal slaughter.

Most of you sense God's presence in some way, or at least you have hope that a higher justice will prevail, and that there may be peace in this life and the next. But how can one follow these goals and at the same time, take part in the killing and maiming of other living entities? A human cannot fully explain the ways of the inconceivable Godhead, but this much is clear: We should not kill unnecessarily, and if we do, we will only bring suffering upon ourselves.

The conscience of the killer (of animals or humans) cannot be at peace. Please do not mock my words, I know I am full of faults. Please do not dispute this human and godly plea: "Do not kill." I am not arguing to defeat anyone, nor do I present myself as an ideal example; I do not seek your votes, nor do I seek power. But I have killed many animals in this lifetime, and only by the grace of my spiritual master have I become free of it. It is therefore my duty to him to speak of this grave subject to others. Had I not stopped killing, I am convinced that I would have had to suffer in the future for the torture I inflicted on others, the dumb creatures of God.

This is the conclusion of the scriptures: Practice *ahiṁsā,* never harm others. Some who profess to follow religion are themselves steeped in blood. They justify the killing of innocent creatures as religious sacrifice, but they are wrong on this point. They are in ignorance.

If you who hear these words are even the least bit inclined to consider them, please try to detach yourselves from participation in this murder. It is quite easy to abandon murder and take up the life of nonviolence. People are taking this step in your own neighborhood. Hear from them and try to see the good in it. Do not mind if others think that you are odd. If you prefer to remain anonymous, you can privately and gradually give up directly killing creatures or buying their flesh for your food.

But do not delay. As for myself, I had a heavy karmic load on my head because I directly broke animals' legs and left them writhing in the forest. Yet even a distant implication or agreement with the act of killing cows and other creatures carries as much responsibility as the killing itself. In this way, karma links up the guilty parties in the conspiracy. Save yourself and break free from it.

Do not face your Maker at the end of life as one who was an enemy of the animals. Do not be deluded that kindness to humans and the killing of animals can go together.

Now that I have been engaged in chanting God's names and am no longer killing, I am a different person; I am peaceful and rectified. Still, I have dreams of the misery I caused others by the misuse of my intelligence and strength. I sometimes dream that the animals I killed are able to testify against me or to directly come and take their revenge. Yes, my dreams are a kind of mental fantasy, but if I had not given up the killing, these dreams would be indications of what is to come for one who kills.

Of course, killing and torturing human beings is even worse, and I do not even address that here as something that needs to be said. No sane person advocates the killing of human beings. And yet if we do not refrain from violence against animals, how will we curb the tendency to be violent against human beings? The same lusts and perverted instincts that convince us to kill animals—that it is in our interest to do so—the same drives and rationalizations lead us to see fellow human beings as enemies and therefore expendable creatures. Violence breeds more violence and creates a karma that will come back on us—as violence upon our own minds and bodies, upon that of our families and upon our land and country, and upon all humankind.

God gives us allotted food, but this does not include wanton slaughter. We may take the production of our agriculture and the milk of the cow (which is her blood transformed, but does not require her death). All our mistakes and persistent impurities can be purified by making offerings of all we eat to the Supreme.

The *sādhus* of Bharata-varśa know this simple method of making devotional offerings of food to God before one eats. The potency of this act is wonderful. When we prepare foods that are acceptable according to the scriptures, and when we offer these foods with prayers of devotion to Bhagavān, then He accepts them. The food is transformed into *prasādam,* "God's mercy," and by eating we can become sanctified, rather than complicated by sin. Lord Kṛṣṇa states in the *Bhagavad-gītā,* "If one offers Me with love and devotion a leaf, a flower, fruit or water, I will accept it." Just by this simple act, we can become pleasing to God; we can never please God by killing (or supporting the killing) of His innocent creatures.

So many bad reactions will occur for animal killing—which is linked up to war, disease, and famine—while all auspiciousness follows the simple act of offering Kṛṣṇa what He desires, and abstaining from meat, fish, and eggs. In this way, we can work toward life's dearmost objective—devotion to God. Who is such a fool that he does not want to be Kṛṣṇa conscious by this simple method, and thus attain the highest perfection, a life of eternity, bliss, and knowledge?

Notes by SDG

Chapter 1

p. 5: The name Viṣṇu-rāta was given to Mahārāja Parīkṣit because he was personally saved by Lord Viṣṇu in the womb of his mother, Uttarā. This is described in the Tenth Canto of *Śrīmad-Bhāgavatam*. Mahārāja Parīkṣit recalls:

> Because my mother surrendered unto Lord Kṛṣṇa's lotus feet, the Lord, *sudarśana-cakra* in hand, entered her womb and saved my body, the body of the last remaining descendant of the Kurus and the Pāṇḍavas, which was almost destroyed by the fiery weapon of Aṣvatthama.
>
> —*Bhāg.* 10.1.5-7

Śrīla Prabhupāda comments that whoever seeks shelter at the lotus feet of the Lord is immediately protected by the Lord. Therefore, everyone can become Viṣṇu-rāta by following Kṛṣṇa's instructions in *Bhagavad-gītā:* "I shall deliver you from all sinful reactions. Do not fear."

p. 6: The biographer describes hunters' lives as sad and wrong. They are *duṣkṛtina,* or impious. On the material side, hunters and animal slaughterers have made tremendous progress since the ancient days. Now by technological methods, millions of animals are killed daily by efficient methods. But even by looking at ordinary statistics, one can see that there has been no moral advancement from the days when hunters and slaughterers wielded only axes and knives and waded in blood.

The term *"duṣkṛtina"* does not negate the fact that a sinful person, like a hunter, may show signs of decent behavior in certain areas. But *duṣkṛtina* means that all the good qualities are ultimately negated or ruined by heavy sinful acts in defiance of the laws of God. One may take care to see that his children are well fed and educated, but then kill the children of other mothers and fathers. In such a case, one may admit that the man was kind to his own children, but his wholesale slaughter of others makes him a hypocrite, a great wrong-doer. These are harsh sounding words, but Vaiṣṇava *ācāryas* like His Divine Grace Śrīla Prabhupāda did not hesitate in "calling a spade a spade." Neither is this criticism of the *duṣkṛtina* meant to be an ultimate condemnation; it is an impetus for devotees to try to save the *duṣkṛtinās.* Prabhupāda's strong words, and the strong words of all Vaiṣṇavas, are intended to wake up those in ignorance.

p. 8-9: The chapter makes brief references to the exalted nature of forest *sādhus.* In the *Śrīmad-Bhāgavatam* and the *Rāmāyaṇa,* there are many portraits of charming hermitages and the clean and pure lives of devotees and transcendentalists who live in the forests of Bharata-varśa. The Six Gosvāmīs of Vṛndāvana lived in the crest jewel of all forests, the forests of Vraja. Materialists like Viṣṇu-rāta's father see such *sādhus* as "doing nothing." But the biographer gives us a moment when we watch Viṣṇu-rāta silently observing a *sādhu* and becoming fascinated by his prayer, even without knowing what the *sādhu* is doing.

If we could study the inner movements of those liberated souls who are no longer dependent on the frenzied activities of material life, we would be attracted to their peaceful state of mind, their devotion to the Supreme Lord, and the fact that they have left behind all material cares. As we shall see in the second chapter, this was the life that Nārada Muni recommended for Mṛgāri. Śrīla Prabhupāda writes:

> . . . One may live in a cave, in a cottage beside a river, in a palace or in a big city like New York or London. In any case, a devotee can follow this instruction of his spiritual master and engage in devotional service by watering the *tulasī* plant and chanting the Hare Kṛṣṇa mantra.
>
> —*Cc. Madhya* 24.261, purport

p. 11-13: The anonymous biographer was eager to introduce the holy names of Rādhā and Kṛṣṇa as soon as possible into this work. Therefore, although there was nothing external in the life of Viṣṇu-rāta to indicate Rādhā-Kṛṣṇa *bhajana,* the biographer has exclaimed about Them, as if he could not keep silent. For one who has realized the ultimate truth as taught by Lord Caitanya and the Six Gosvāmīs, what is the use of a spiritual narration unless one can come to the point of glorifying Rādhā-Kṛṣṇa? Even the noble cause of *ahiṁsā* remains incomplete unless we go further and finally speak of and serve Rādhā-Kṛṣṇa.

p. 16: The biographer tells us that Viṣṇu-rāta's activities were not divine *līlā.* This indicates that by the grace of his spiritual master, he had to make advancement in Kṛṣṇa consciousness by the method of *sādhana-bhakti.* A person may commit sinful activities, but upon receiving the grace of the Vaiṣṇavas and taking up Kṛṣṇa consciousness, he can gradually rid himself of all traces of sin. By the power of *bhakti-yoga,* the *sādhana-siddha* devotee can become equal in purity and devotion to the person who is eternally liberated *(nitya-siddha).*

p. 17-19: When he was a very young child, Viṣṇu-rāta did not make any emotional connection between the meat he was served at mealtime and the living creatures who had to give their lives to become his "veal cutlet." Nowadays, modern advertising has pushed this ignorance to the extremes of perversity. Many restaurants show happy cartoon pictures of the cow or chicken served inside. The general populace has been driven to such a point of inanity that without thinking, everyone joins in the spirit, amused at the happy cow who is dancing and smiling from the sizzling frying pan, or the chicken with the bow tie, etc. By the propaganda of those who advocate *ahiṁsā,* as well as by the fact that the ill effects of meat-eating will become more and more pronounced, the day may come when the government will require advertisers to state the actual horrible effects of animal slaughter and meat-eating. If the billboards showed the real picture of what went on in the slaughterhouse instead of the animated cartoon, then people might be dissuaded from living in such illusion, and come to their senses about meat-eating.

p. 20-1: Viṣṇu-rāta's mother gives a series of arguments why it is all right to eat meat. She refers to a śāstric statement that one living being is food for another. Śrīla Prabhupāda has explained that this is the law for animals, but that human beings should be better than animals. A human is a type of animal, but he is also a human. If a human is in no way different from the animals, then he is most degraded. Viṣṇu-rāta's mother's arguments are mostly false assurances, "There is nothing to be afraid of. . . . These are the facts of life."

Of course, when children of meat-eaters hear these instructions from their parents, they are often convinced, even though the "arguments" have no basis in fact and are ignorant of the law of karma. Throughout the chapter, we also hear several references to Viṣṇu-rāta's father deliberately avoiding the subject of karma. As Prabhupāda has said, if the materialist could actually understand karma and the next life, he would shudder and be unable to enjoy himself.

Chapter 2:

p. 32-3: Although Śrīla Prabhupāda strongly advocates that devotees in the Kṛṣṇa consciousness movement should preach, he sometimes describes a kind of simple, retired life in the forest which some Vaiṣṇavas have chosen as their way. In the case of Mṛgāri, Nārada gave him specific instructions to build a simple cottage, live there with his wife on the bank of a the holy river, and incessantly chant the Hare Kṛṣṇa mantra. In his purport, Prabhupāda gives directions for building a cottage, as if he were giving practical advice for someone interested in this way of life:

> Four logs serving as pillars can be secured by any man from the forest. The roof can be covered with leaves, and one can cleanse the inside. Thus one can live very peacefully. In any condition, any man can live in a small cottage, plant a *tulasī* tree, water it in the morning, offer it prayers and continuously chant the Hare Kṛṣṇa *mahā-mantra.* Thus one can make vigorous spiritual advancement. This is not at all difficult. . . . One may live in a cave, in a cottage beside a river, in a palace or in a big city like New York or London. In any case, a devotee can follow this instruction of his spiritual master and engage in devotional service by watering the *tulasī* plant and chanting the Hare Kṛṣṇa mantra.
>
> —*Cc. Madhya* 24.261, purport

p. 33: Prabhupāda advises devotees not to keep a stock of food for the next day. He writes, "We should not materially calculate, thinking, 'It is better to stock food for a week. Why give the Lord trouble by having Him bring food daily?' One should be convinced that the Lord will provide it daily. There is no need to stock food for the next day" (*Cc. Madhya* 24.280, purport).

Of course, these instructions have to be understood in a particular context. They are instructions for renounced persons. Obviously, devotees maintaining a big institution with many members would have to keep a stock of food, both for the inmates as well as for opulent worship of the Deity and for public *prasādam* distribution. Our point in mentioning it here is to appreciate that Prabhupāda has more than one mood, and more than one set of instructions. Here he clearly says that Lord Caitanya's instruction is not to stock food, and that a *gṛhastha* can make vigorous spiritual advancement by living in a very simple cottage and spending all his time chanting Hare Kṛṣṇa.

p. 34: The footnote by Vaiṣṇava-dāsānu dāsa mentions that the anonymous biographer is sometimes expressing his own ideas and sometimes adhering strictly to the narration. Although he has occasionally interjected his own opinions or evaluations into the manuscript, Vaiṣṇava-dāsānu dāsa assures us that we can trust the biographer to alert us to any additions to the text. This practice is common among Vaiṣṇava writers, but whatever additions they make are sure to be in line with the *paramparā*.

Mundane authors cannot appreciate the strength that comes from writing or reading in Vaiṣṇava *paramparā.* Those who do not write in *paramparā* think themselves original and free, although they may acknowledge various influences. A Vaiṣṇava author is one who realizes that his own fertile brain is extremely limited and faulty. He thinks, "What is the use of my expressing my own ideas since I am only a tiny creature who has been forced to come into this world and who does not know anything beyond a very tiny scope?" He therefore links up to the line of liberated *ācāryas.* He receives knowledge coming down from the Supreme Lord, who blesses sincere devotees and awakens revelation in their hearts.

This does not mean that a Vaiṣṇava loses his originality, unique voice, thinking power, and so on. But he contributes whatever he has, considering it God-given, to the cause of Vaiṣṇava *siddhānta,* and thus he can create lasting works—works that can actually help people, not merely entertain them or give them a sense of kinship without ultimate victory.

p. 35-44: The biographer's account of the first meeting between Viṣṇu-rāta and his spiritual master, the ex-hunter Mṛgāri, sounds similar on some points to the first meeting of His Divine Grace A.C. Bhaktivedanta Swami Prabhupāda with his spiritual master, Śrīla Bhaktisiddhānta Sarasvatī Ṭhākura Prabhupāda. The meeting of a sincere disciple with his eternal spiritual master is a kind of love story of spiritual life. It occurs in the life of every devotee. Each case is unique, but there are bound to be many similarities. Those who value spiritual life and who are aware of the necessity of the guru-disciple relationship, like to hear genuine accounts of meetings of disciples with their spiritual masters. As the materialists do not tire of hearing many varieties on the "boy-meets-girl" theme, the spiritualists take pleasure in hearing firsthand accounts by persons who were saved from the "well" of material life by receiving the mercy of a Vaiṣṇava spiritual master. It is the recurring theme of how God's mercy appears in the world.

Chapter 3:

p. 52: Mṛgāri was disturbed about breaking his bow because he was worried about his income. Nārada Muni assured him that Kṛṣṇa would supply his food. When Mṛgāri followed Nārada's instructions, the villagers began to bring alms and present them to the Vaiṣṇava who was formerly a hunter.

Śrīla Prabhupāda affirms that Kṛṣṇa is ready to supply all of life's necessities, provided a Vaiṣṇava follows the principles set forth by the spiritual master. But Śrīla Prabhupāda warns devotees not to take advantage of Kṛṣṇa, or of the pious public, and lead a lazy life, seeking support in the name of religion. Prabhupāda writes, "A temple should not be a place to eat and sleep. A temple manager should be very careful about these things" *(Cc. Madhya* 24.266, purport). This advice applies both to married persons *(gṛhasthas)* as well as those in the renounced order *(sannyāsīs)*. Whether one chooses to maintain himself by business earnings or to live as a mendicant and accept alms, all are ultimately dependent on Kṛṣṇa, and all devotees should fully engage themselves in some sort of devotional service. In the case of Mṛgāri, he gave up hunting and became a full-time chanter of the holy name. Although Nārada assured him that he would send sufficient food, he also advised the hunter "to accept only what is absolutely necessary for him and his wife. The devotee should always be alert to consume only those things that he actually requires and not create unnecessary needs" *(Cc. Madhya,* 24.262, purport).

It is not fair to interpret the story of Mṛgāri the hunter as an example of a productive worker who later became a lazy parasite. Neither are the verses and purports intended as criticism toward *gṛhasthas* who earn incomes and live outside temples. Everyone should know that our maintenance in life depends on Kṛṣṇa, and everyone should chant His holy names as much as possible.

p. 53-5: Nārada-kṛpa Prabhu declares that he is chanting in the *nāma-bhasa,* or clearing stage. One may take this as a humble statement, or one may be doubtful how a chanter who has not reached *śuddha-nāma,* or chanting in pure love of God, can be a spiritual advisor. As Nārada-kṛpa states, even a beginner attains the presence of Kṛṣṇa in His holy name. One may still be struggling to control one's mind, and therefore sometimes guilty of inattention, an offense in chanting. But if one goes on chanting wholeheartedly despite his faults, then his "struggle" is glorious. Everyone can learn from such a staunch example.

And who can argue against the genuine realization of Nārada-kṛpa: "I am eager to go on chanting and experiencing the further stages. But basically I chant under the order of my *guru mahārāja,* Nārada, and I am happy for the first time in my life"? Nārada-kṛpa demonstrates his faith in the holy name by repeatedly advising his new friend, Viṣṇu-rāta, that the formidable obstacles on his path, such as opposition from his father, will be cleared up by the Supreme Lord's intervention—if Viṣṇu-rāta simply persists in chanting.

p. 56: We previously mentioned that the first meeting of a sincere disciple and his eternal spiritual master is like a timeless love story that has been told and retold in many personal histories, and which never fails to inspire serious transcendentalists. The story of troubles encountered by new devotees whose parents are opposed to Kṛṣṇa consciousness is also an old story and has occurred throughout the centuries in many cultures and religions of the world. It is not an absolute principle that all parents will be opposed, or that the young disciple should meet that opposition by disobedience to parental orders. But a new devotee should at least be assured that he is not the first person in history to face this trouble. Many have faced the test and passed it. But it requires patience, tact, compassion, and strong determination as each person faces the test for himself or herself.

In the case of Śrī Caitanya Mahāprabhu, whose *līlā* was to appear as a human being in West Bengal, He also broke from home, leaving at night and abandoning His young wife and mother in order to take *sannyāsa*. In His case, His mother and wife continued to worship Him and did not disturb His *sannyāsa* vows.

Viṣṇu-rāta's relationship with his father is an extreme example of the opposition of a son and his father. In the beginning, Viṣṇu-rāta's motives are mixed between his strong desire for liberation in Kṛṣṇa consciousness, and his rebellion against an unreasonable and dominating father.

p. 63: The policeman of Viṣṇu-rāta's village advises the young man that all occupations are valid. His statement that any profession may have imperfections, just as fire sometimes has smoke, is a parallel of Lord Kṛṣṇa's teachings in *Bhagavad-gītā*. But Lord Kṛṣṇa does not say that even forbidden works should be pursued despite their imperfections. If one is engaged in *ugrā-karma,* sinful work, especially work that causes unnecessary pain and death to others, then that work cannot be justified on the principle that "there is always some fault in every endeavor, but don't renounce it." The desperate work of the *asuras* is condemned in the sixteenth chapter of *Bhagavad-gītā.*

Nārada even makes a distinction between hunting animals, which he considers a "slight offense," and the torture of the animals in leaving them half-dead, which he strongly deplores. Nārada says, "I beg you from this day on that you will kill animals completely and not leave them half-dead." Similarly, there is a distinction between a hunter of olden days who went out into the woods and killed animals for his maintenance, and the modern-day slaughterhouse. Both the olden day hunter and the modern-day slaughterhouse operators must face punishment for their deeds, but the wholesale production line slaughtering is much worse.

> Although the hunter Mṛgāri was uncivilized, he still had to suffer the results of his sinful activities. However, if a civilized man kills animals regularly in a slaughterhouse to maintain his so-called civilization, using scientific methods and machines to kill animals, one cannot even estimate the suffering awaiting him.
>
> —*Cc. Madhya* 24. 249, purport

The only killing of animals that is sanctioned in Vedic culture is that which is done in sacrifice to the Goddess Kālī or a similar demigod or demigoddess. These sacrifices are generally performed only once a month and with stringent restrictions. Prabhupāda writes, "Even by following this method, one is still an offender." But nowadays, civilized societies do not sacrifice animals to deities in a religious or ritualistic way. Prabhupāda writes further, "They openly kill animals daily by the thousands for no purpose other than the satisfaction of the tongue. Because of this, the entire world is suffering in so many ways. Politicians are unnecessarily declaring war, and according to the stringent laws of material nature, massacres are taking place between nations" (*Cc. Madhya,* 24.250, purport).

p.63: The policeman's moralizing about the validity of a hunter's life suggests sanction by legal and religious authorities. In his purports to this section of *Caitanya-caritāmṛta,* Śrīla Prabhupāda exposes "rascals" who violate their own religious principles and give support to animal-killing.

> According to Judeo-Christian scriptures, it is clearly said, "Thou shalt not kill." Nonetheless, giving all kinds of excuses, even the heads of religions indulge in killing animals while trying to pass as saintly persons. This mockery and hypocrisy in human society brings about unlimited calamities.
>
> —*Cc. Madhya* 24.251, purport

Chapter 4:

p. 67: Viṣṇu-rāta offers the argument that he has bad character traits because of his environment and upbringing. This is no doubt true, yet a person also has the capacity to remove himself from bad association, provided he gets the fortune to meet genuine Vaiṣṇavas. Every conditioned soul comes to this world by his own karma, and by free will we may again turn to Kṛṣṇa. So Viṣṇu-rāta's "environment theory" (shared by some modern sociologists) is incomplete.

Moreover, even if one is lowborn and ill-trained, he can become elevated and purified by right association with spiritually-minded persons. There are many examples in the scriptures of this. No one should feel inferior because of his birth and upbringing. But those who seek to uplift humanity cannot simply rubber-stamp people as *"harijanas"* and think that the job is finished. Those who are considered lowborn in society must actually learn and practice right behavior in order to become something different and better.

p. 67: Viṣṇu-rāta admits that anger is so dangerous that he and his father might have killed each other in a sudden brawl. Śrīla Prabhupāda also mentioned in a 1968 lecture on the yoga system, that all transcendentalists must control their anger. Prabhupāda said that anger is so dangerous that in a moment of rage, one may kill one's "own men." In the *Bhagavad-gītā,* Kṛṣṇa explains that when lust is frustrated, wrath appears. Anger is therefore the "younger brother" of material desire. Anger is an *anārtha* that Viṣṇu-rāta must seek to remove. At the end of this chapter, he receives a dream-inspiration of how he may dovetail his anger in the service of nonviolence.

p. 67: Under the direction of Nārada Muni, Mṛgāri gave up his occupation as a hunter. Viṣṇu-rāta is prepared to do the same. But what if everyone gave up their jobs and became mendicants chanting Hare Kṛṣṇa? When Śrīla Prabhupāda was asked this question, he would sometimes reply, "Don't worry, it will never happen." Few people are actually interested in taking wholeheartedly to Kṛṣṇa consciousness and depending on Kṛṣṇa for maintenance. If the world were to become Kṛṣṇa conscious, there would still be people who would work in different occupations according to their tendencies. And if some occupations disappeared from the earth, such as the occupations of thief, murderer, or hunter, what would be the loss?

p. 67: Viṣṇu-rāta asked Nārada-kṛpa how Nārada Muni convinced him to become a devotee. A disciple is always interested in hearing about the life of his spiritual master, from a spiritual point of view. Similarly, Vyāsadeva asked Nārada how he grew up and developed his Kṛṣṇa consciousness. Nārada's origins, as described in the First Canto of *Śrīmad-Bhāgavatam,* were humble. He was the son of a maidservant, and his story of "how I came to Kṛṣṇa consciousness" is one of the most wonderful of all.

p. 73: The description of the animals who fearlessly entered Nārada-kṛpa's cottage gives a hint of a world in which humans and animals might live at peace. Kṛṣṇaloka is such a place, where even animals who are constitutionally inimical to humans live in loving relationship with Kṛṣṇa. The *Bhāgavatam* describes:

> Vṛndāvana is the transcendental abode of the Lord, where there is no hunger, anger or thirst. Though naturally inimical, both human beings and fierce animals live there together in transcendental friendship.
>
> —*Bhāg.* 10.13.60

There are also true accounts of sages living in the forest who developed friendly relationships with tigers. The sages would leave milk at some distant place. They would then call for the tigers the way one calls for a domestic cat. The tigers would come and drink the milk and never harm the sages. The Supersoul who is also present in the ferocious animals, would dictate to them not to harm the sages, and not to fear anything from them.

p. 77-79: Viṣṇu-rāta's taking action on the basis of his dream shows him to be impetuous. Often people would ask Śrīla Prabhupāda how they should take their dreams in which Kṛṣṇa appeared to them and in which they got various instructions. Prabhupāda said that everything should be corroborated with guru, *śāstra,* and *sādhu.*

Chapter 5:

p. 81-82: Viṣṇu-rāta's impetuous plans to protect the animals seem to include the possibility of meeting violence with violence. In the *Bhagavad-gītā*, when Lord Kṛṣṇa orders Arjuna to fight, Śrīla Prabhupāda comments: "When Kṛṣṇa orders fighting, it must be concluded that violence is for supreme justice, and thus Arjuna should follow the instruction, knowing well that such violence, committed in the act of fighting for Kṛṣṇa, is not violence at all. . . " *(Bg.* 2.21). But one cannot whimsically commit violence and justify it as coming from God or as necessary for some other just cause.

p. 84: Ambulal, the son of the utensil maker, argues that the killing of vegetables is just as bad as the killing of animals. I recall this same question being asked by Greg Scharf (later initiated as Gargamuni dāsa) of Śrīla Prabhupāda in 1966. Prabhupāda smiled and replied, "That is a very intelligent question." Prabhupāda then explained that Kṛṣṇa conscious persons are not, strictly speaking, vegetarians. Their eating habits are determined by the principle that all food should be offered first to the Lord. The devotee eats only remnants of food offered to Kṛṣṇa because he wishes to develop his devotion to the Lord in every act of life. Kṛṣṇa specifically says in the *Bhagavad-gītā* that He accepts a leaf or fruit or water when it is offered with devotion. Kṛṣṇa does not want animals to be killed and offered to Him in the name of *prasādam*. And that is why the devotees are vegetarians.

Śrīla Prabhupāda has also pointed out that in many cases, the taking of vegetarian foods does not kill the living entity. One may take apples from the tree without hurting the tree. In the case of wheat, the plant produces the ripe grain, and then immediately dies. But even if we argue that some vegetables must be killed in order to be eaten, there is still a difference between eating a carrot and eating the flesh of a cow. Even a meat-eater makes a distinction between eating human flesh and eating cow flesh. The vegetables have been given to the human being as their allotted food.

The physical constitution of the human being also reveals his innate vegetarianism. If one compares the teeth and digestive system of a human with the teeth and digestive system of a carnivore, one can see the marked difference. But Ambulal is correct in saying that vegetarians must also take life to eat. Therefore, in order to absolve ourselves from bad karma, even strict vegetarians must offer their food to Kṛṣṇa in sacrifice. That act absolves one from sin. Kṛṣṇa states, "The devotees of the Lord are released from all kinds of sins because they eat food which is offered first in sacrifice. Others, who prepare food for personal sense enjoyment, verily eat only sin" *(Bg.* 3.13).

p. 89-91: The policeman suggests that Viṣṇu-rāta could better engage himself in the cause of animal protection and nonviolence by becoming a *sādhu* and a preacher rather than by engaging in hand-to-hand combat with the hunters. There is some worldly compromise in the words of the policeman, but he is well-intentioned toward Viṣṇu-rāta, and he appreciates the role of the *sādhu* in promoting nonviolence in society.

Śrīla Prabhupāda has fully explained the nature of peaceful nonviolence in its highest sense:

> People in general are trapped by ignorance in the material concept of life, and they perpetually suffer material pains. So unless one elevates people to spiritual knowledge, one is practicing violence. One should try his best to distribute real knowledge to the people, so that they might become enlightened and leave this material entanglement. That is nonviolence.
>
> —*Bg.* 13.8-12, purport

Chapter 6:

p. 92: Viṣṇu-rāta realizes that he has failed because of not taking direction from the spiritual master. When we follow a bona fide spiritual master, then we have great strength behind us—all of the *ācāryas* in disciplic succession and Lord Kṛṣṇa Himself. When we act without connection to our spiritual master, then we are all alone—a dangerous and weak position. When we are alone, we speculate based on our limited powers as to what is right and wrong. When one acts under the instructions of the spiritual master, he can perform wonderful feats.

Śrīla Prabhupāda said that he did not consider himself a great scholar or a great devotee, but his one claim was that he had one hundred percent faith in his spiritual master and carried out his instructions wholeheartedly. "By the blessings of the spiritual master the lame man can cross mountains, the dumb man can speak like a great orator, and a blind man can see the stars in the sky."

p. 92: Nārada-kṛpa Prabhu acknowledged that a devotee may receive subtle karmic reactions in the form of dreams. This point of view is confirmed in a *Śrīmad-Bhāgavatam* verse and purport:

Translation:

> Kṛṣṇa consciousness means constantly associating with the Supreme Personality of Godhead in such a mental state that the devotee can observe the cosmic manifestation exactly as the Supreme Personality of Godhead does. Such observation is not always possible, but it becomes manifest exactly like the dark planet known as Rāhu, which is observed in the presence of the full moon.

Purport:

> It has been explained in the previous verse that all desires on the mental platform become visible one after another. Sometimes, however, by the supreme will of the Supreme Personality of Godhead, the whole stockpile can be visible all at one time. In *Brahma-saṁhitā* (5.54) it is said, *karmāṇi nirdahati kintu ca bhakti-bhājām.* When a person is fully absorbed in Kṛṣṇa consciousness, his stockpile of material desires is minimized. Indeed, the desires no longer fructify in the form of

gross bodies. Instead, the stockpile of desires becomes visible on the mental platform by the grace of the Supreme Personality of Godhead. . . . The point is that a living entity has immense and unlimited desires for material enjoyment, and he has to transmigrate from one gross body to another until these desires are exhausted.

No living entity is free from the cycle of birth and death unless he takes to Kṛṣṇa consciousness; therefore . . . when one is fully absorbed in Kṛṣṇa consciousness, in one stroke he is freed of past and future mental desires. Then, by the grace of the Supreme Lord, everything becomes simultaneously manifest within the mind. . . . A Kṛṣṇa conscious person can see all his dormant desires at one time and finish all his future transmigrations. This facility is especially given to the devotee to make his path clear for returning home, back to Godhead.

—*Bhāg.* 4.29.69

Glossary

A

ācamana—to purify with water. Before offering something to the Deity or Tulasī plant, one washes one's hand with a few drops of water.

ācamana cup—a small metal cup (and spoon) placed near an altar or place of worship for purifying the hands.

ācārya—a spiritual master who teaches by example.

Age of Kali—see Kali-yuga.

ahiṁsa—nonviolence.

āśrama—the four spiritual orders of life: celibate student, householder, retired, and renounced life. Also, a dwelling place for spiritual shelter.

asura—a demon; a person with demoniac qualities.

attar—a spicy pickle usually eaten with meals in India.

B

bhagavata-dharma—one's eternal duty of serving the Supreme Lord.

bhakti-yoga—linking with the Supreme Lord through devotional service.

Bharata-varśa—the land of India.

bidi—an Indian cigarette.

C

cādar—a blanket-like wrap worn around the shoulders.

capātī—a flat, unleavened bread, commonly eaten in northern India.

D

daṇḍa—a rod carried by persons in the renounced order.

daṇḍavats—literally, "falling down like a rod"; offering prostrated obeisances.

darśana—literally, to see. An audience with a saintly person or with the Deity.

deva deva jagat pate—the God of all gods and the Lord of the whole universe.

dhāma—abode, place of residence, usually referring to the Lord's abode.

dharma—(1) religious principles; (2) one's eternal, natural occupation (ie., devotional service to the Lord).

dhotī—lower garment worn by men in India.

duṣkṛtina—an impious person given to sinful activity.

G

Goddess Kālī—another name for Dūrga; goddess in charge of the material energy.

gosvāmī—literally, controller of the senses. A person in the renounced order of life.

gṛhastha—regulated householder life; the second order of Vedic spiritual life.

guru mahārāja—a generic title for the spiritual master.

H

harijana—literally, a son of God (Hari).

harināma—congregational chanting of the Lord's holy names.

J

japa—soft, private chanting of the holy names, usually done on beads.

K

Kali-yuga—The Age of Kali; the present age, characterized by quarrel; it is the last in the cycle of four ages and began five thousand years ago.

karma—fruitive action, for which there is always reaction, good or bad.

kichari—a rice and bean combination cooked together like a wholesome stew.

kī jaya—literally, victory!

kīrtana—chanting the glories of the Supreme Lord.

kṛṣṇa-prema—the highest love of God.

L

līlā—pastime.

M

mahā-harināma—a large congregation of chanters singing the holy names of the Lord. *Mahā*—great, large.

mahā-prasādam—food offered to the Deity.

mantra—a sound vibration that can deliver the mind from illusion.

marā—death.

māyā—(*mā*-not; *yā*-this), illusion; forgetfulness of one's relationship with Kṛṣṇa.

P

paśandi—an animal-like person.

pūjā—worship.

R

rajo-guṇa—the material mode of passion.

Rāmāyāna—a book about the pastimes of Lord Rāmacandra, written by the great sage Vālmikī.

S

sādhana—regulated spiritual practices.

sādhana-siddha—a devotee who has perfected himself or herself through the practice of *sādhana.*

śaktyāveṣa-avatāra—a liberated soul who is directly empowered by the Lord to perform a mission in the material world.

sādhu-saṅga—association of saintly persons.

śaligrama-śila—a Deity of Kṛṣṇa in the form of a stone.

sannyāsī—a person in the renounced order of life, the fourth spiritual order in Vedic society.

śāstra—revealed scripture.

siddhānta—the revealed truth of the scriptures; the essence.

sparśa-maṇi—a touchstone. A saintly person who, simply by his association, awakens one's dormant Kṛṣṇa consciousness.

T

tamo-guṇa—the material mode of ignorance.

tilaka—clay markings worn on the forehead and other parts of the body to signify devotion to a particular religion. Vaiṣṇava *tilaka* is signified by two parallel lines going up from the bridge of the nose to the hairline.

tri-veṇī—the confluence of three rivers, the Ganges, Yamunā, and the Sarasvatī at Prayāga.

V

Vaiṣṇava—literally, a worshiper of Lord Viṣṇu; a devotee of Kṛṣṇa.

varṇa—occupation.

Vedas—the four original scriptures.

vīṇā—a stringed musical instrument played in India.

I would like to thank the following disciples and friends for helping to produce and print this book: Caitanya-rūpa-devī dāsī, Madana-mohana dāsa, Kaiśorī-devī dāsī, Yadupriyā-devī dāsī and Vegavatī-devī dāsī. Special thanks to Himavatī-devī dāsī for her kind donation to print this book.

Other Books by Satsvarūpa dāsa Goswami

Readings in Vedic Literature
A Handbook for Kṛṣṇa Consciousness
He Lives Forever
Śrīla Prabhupāda-līlāmṛta (Vols. 1-6)
Distribute Books, Distribute Books, Distribute Books
The Twenty-six Qualities of a Devotee/
Vaiṣṇava Behavior
With Śrīla Prabhupāda in the Early Days: A Memoir (formerly titled: Letters From Śrīla Prabhupāda)
Japa Reform Notebook
The Voices of Surrender and Other Poems
Remembering Śrīla Prabhupāda (Vols. 1-5)
Life With the Perfect Master
In Praise of the Mahājanas and Other Poems
Prabhupāda Nectar (Vols. 1-5)
Living With the Scriptures
Reading Reform Notebook
The Worshipable Deity and Other Poems
Under the Banyan Tree
Dust of Vṛndāvana
Journal and Poems (Books 1-3)
Guru Reform Notebook

(other books cont.)
Prabhupāda-līlā
Pictures From the Bhagavad-gītā As It Is and Other Poems
Lessons From the Road (Vols. 1-17)
Iṣṭa-goṣṭhī (Vols. 1-3)
Nimāi dāsa and the Mouse: A Fable
Nimāi's Detour
Gurudeva and Nimāi: Struggling for Survival
Choṭa's Way
Truthfulness, The Last Leg of Religion
Prabhupāda Meditations (Vols. 1-3)
Prabhupāda Appreciation
ISKCON in the 1970s: Diaries (Vol. 1 & 2)
Memory in the Service of Kṛṣṇa
Obstacles on the Path of Devotional Service
Talking Freely With My Lords
Am I a Demon or a Vaiṣṇava? (Vol. 1 of Stories of Devotion)
My Search Through Books